3/18

DATE DUE

AUG 2 2 2018	
SEP 0 5 2018	
SEP 1 0 2019	

BRODART, CO. Cat. No. 23-221

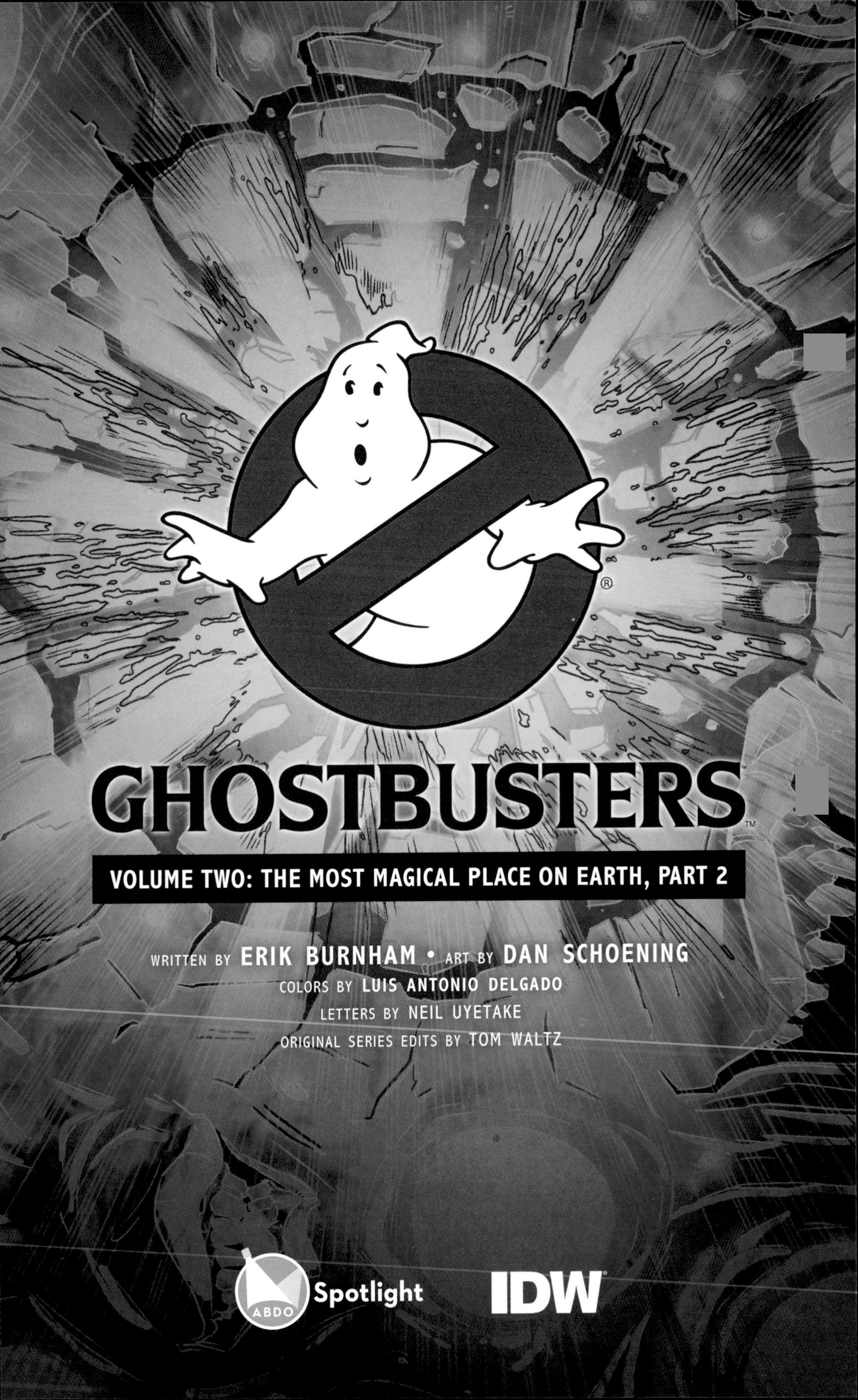

GHOSTBUSTERS™

VOLUME TWO: THE MOST MAGICAL PLACE ON EARTH, PART 2

WRITTEN BY **ERIK BURNHAM** • ART BY **DAN SCHOENING**

COLORS BY **LUIS ANTONIO DELGADO**

LETTERS BY NEIL UYETAKE

ORIGINAL SERIES EDITS BY TOM WALTZ

Spotlight

IDW

ABDOPUBLISHING.COM

Reinforced library bound edition published in 2017 by Spotlight, a division of ABDO
PO Box 398166, Minneapolis, Minnesota 55439. Spotlight produces high-quality
reinforced library bound editions for schools and libraries.
Published by agreement with IDW.

Printed in the United States of America, North Mankato, Minnesota.
042016
092016

THIS BOOK CONTAINS
RECYCLED MATERIALS

IDW

GHOSTBUSTERS, VOLUME 2: THE MOST MAGICAL PLACE ON EARTH. JULY 2012.
FIRST PRINTING. Ghostbusters TM & © 2016 Columbia Pictures, Inc. All rights reserved.
IDW Publishing, a division of Idea and Design Works, LLC. Editorial offices: 5080 Santa Fe St.,
San Diego, CA 92109. The IDW logo is registered in the U.S. Patent and Trademark Office.
Any similarities to persons living or dead are purely coincidental. With the exception of artwork
used for review purposes, none of the contents of this publication may be reprinted without the
permission of Idea and Design Works, LLC. IDW Publishing does not read or accept unsolicited
submissions of ideas, stories, or artwork.

Originally published as GHOSTBUSTERS Issues #5–8.

LIBRARY OF CONGRESS CATALOGING-IN-PUBLICATION DATA

Names: Burnham, Eric, author. | Schoening, Dan, illustrator.
Title: Ghostbusters. Volume 2, The most magical place on earth / writer: Erik Burnham ; art: Dan
    Schoening ; colors: Luis Antonio Delgado.
Other titles: Most magical place on earth
Description: Reinforced library bound edition. | Minneapolis, Minnesota : Spotlight, 2017.
Identifiers: LCCN 2015050200| ISBN 9781614794899 (volume 1) | ISBN 9781614794905 (volume 2)
    | ISBN 9781614794912 (volume 3) | ISBN 9781614794929 (volume 4)
Subjects: LCSH: Graphic novels. | CYAC: Graphic novels.
Classification: LCC PZ7.7.B88 Ghq 2016 | DDC 741.5/973--dc23
LC record available at https://lccn.loc.gov/2015050200

Spotlight

A Division of ABDO
abdopublishing.com

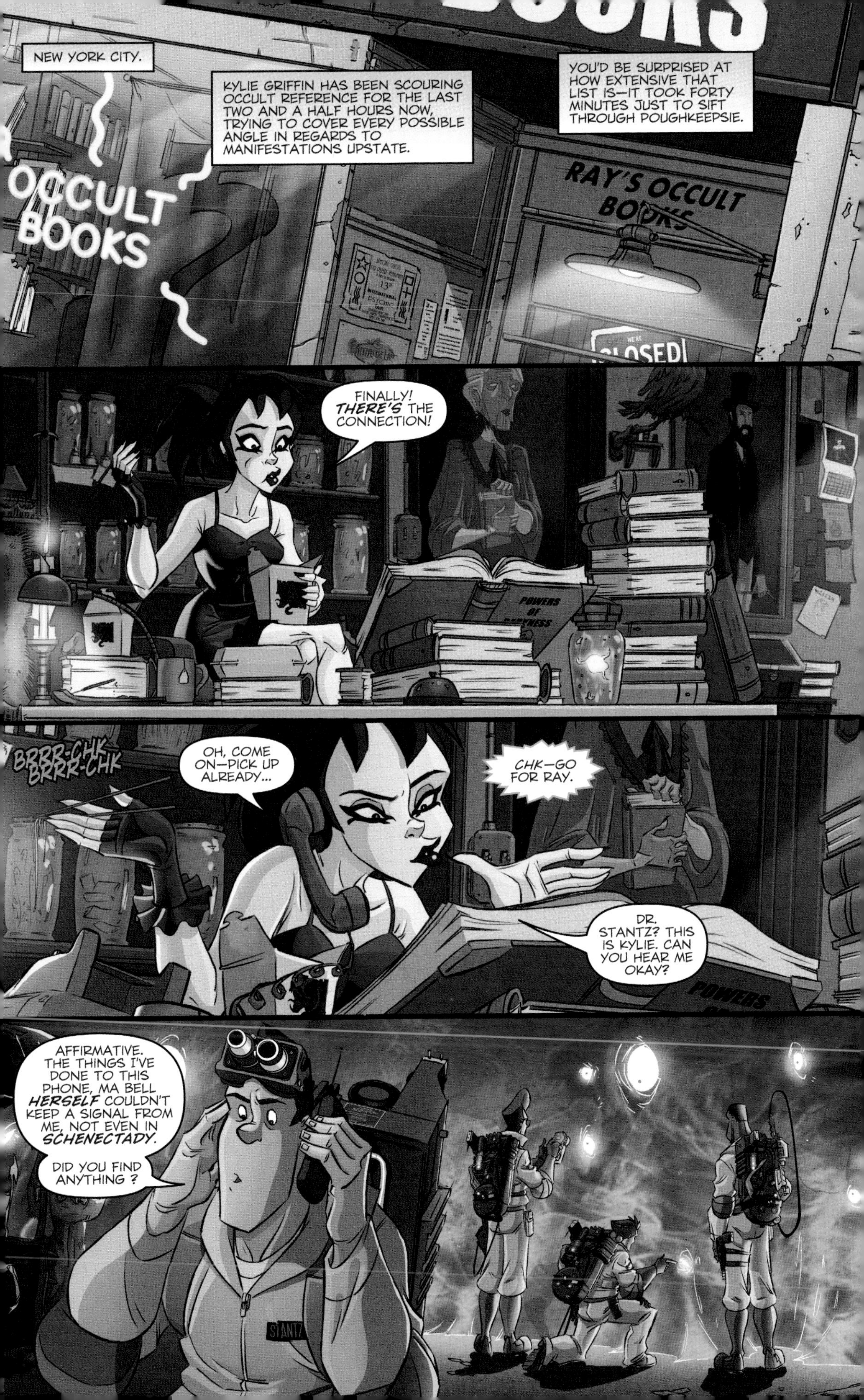

NEW YORK CITY.
KYLIE GRIFFIN HAS BEEN SCOURING OCCULT REFERENCE FOR THE LAST TWO AND A HALF HOURS NOW, TRYING TO COVER EVERY POSSIBLE ANGLE IN REGARDS TO MANIFESTATIONS UPSTATE.
YOU'D BE SURPRISED AT HOW EXTENSIVE THAT LIST IS—IT TOOK FORTY MINUTES JUST TO SIFT THROUGH POUGHKEEPSIE.
OCCULT BOOKS
RAY'S OCCULT BOOKS
CLOSED
FINALLY! THERE'S THE CONNECTION!
POWERS OF
BRRR-CHK BRRR-CHK
OH, COME ON—PICK UP ALREADY...
CHK—GO FOR RAY.
DR. STANTZ? THIS IS KYLIE. CAN YOU HEAR ME OKAY?
POWERS
AFFIRMATIVE. THE THINGS I'VE DONE TO THIS PHONE, MA BELL HERSELF COULDN'T KEEP A SIGNAL FROM ME, NOT EVEN IN SCHENECTADY.
DID YOU FIND ANYTHING ?
STANTZ

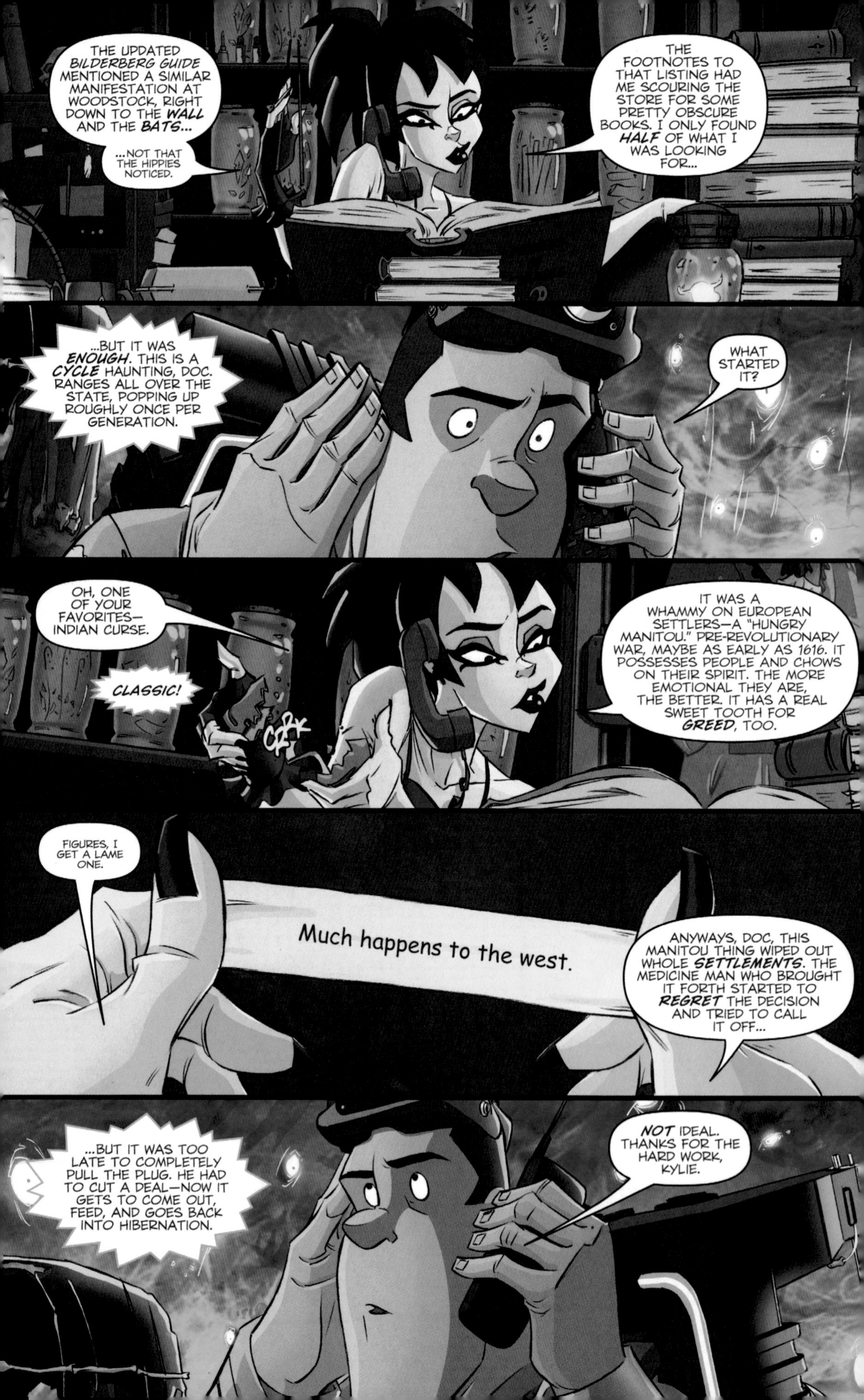
THE UPDATED BILDERBERG GUIDE MENTIONED A SIMILAR MANIFESTATION AT WOODSTOCK, RIGHT DOWN TO THE WALL AND THE BATS...
...NOT THAT THE HIPPIES NOTICED.
THE FOOTNOTES TO THAT LISTING HAD ME SCOURING THE STORE FOR SOME PRETTY OBSCURE BOOKS. I ONLY FOUND HALF OF WHAT I WAS LOOKING FOR...
...BUT IT WAS ENOUGH. THIS IS A CYCLE HAUNTING, DOC. RANGES ALL OVER THE STATE, POPPING UP ROUGHLY ONCE PER GENERATION.
WHAT STARTED IT?
OH, ONE OF YOUR FAVORITES—INDIAN CURSE.
CLASSIC!
CRAK
IT WAS A WHAMMY ON EUROPEAN SETTLERS—A "HUNGRY MANITOU." PRE-REVOLUTIONARY WAR, MAYBE AS EARLY AS 1616. IT POSSESSES PEOPLE AND CHOWS ON THEIR SPIRIT. THE MORE EMOTIONAL THEY ARE, THE BETTER. IT HAS A REAL SWEET TOOTH FOR GREED, TOO.
FIGURES, I GET A LAME ONE.
Much happens to the west.
ANYWAYS, DOC, THIS MANITOU THING WIPED OUT WHOLE SETTLEMENTS. THE MEDICINE MAN WHO BROUGHT IT FORTH STARTED TO REGRET THE DECISION AND TRIED TO CALL IT OFF...
...BUT IT WAS TOO LATE TO COMPLETELY PULL THE PLUG. HE HAD TO CUT A DEAL—NOW IT GETS TO COME OUT, FEED, AND GOES BACK INTO HIBERNATION.
NOT IDEAL. THANKS FOR THE HARD WORK, KYLIE.

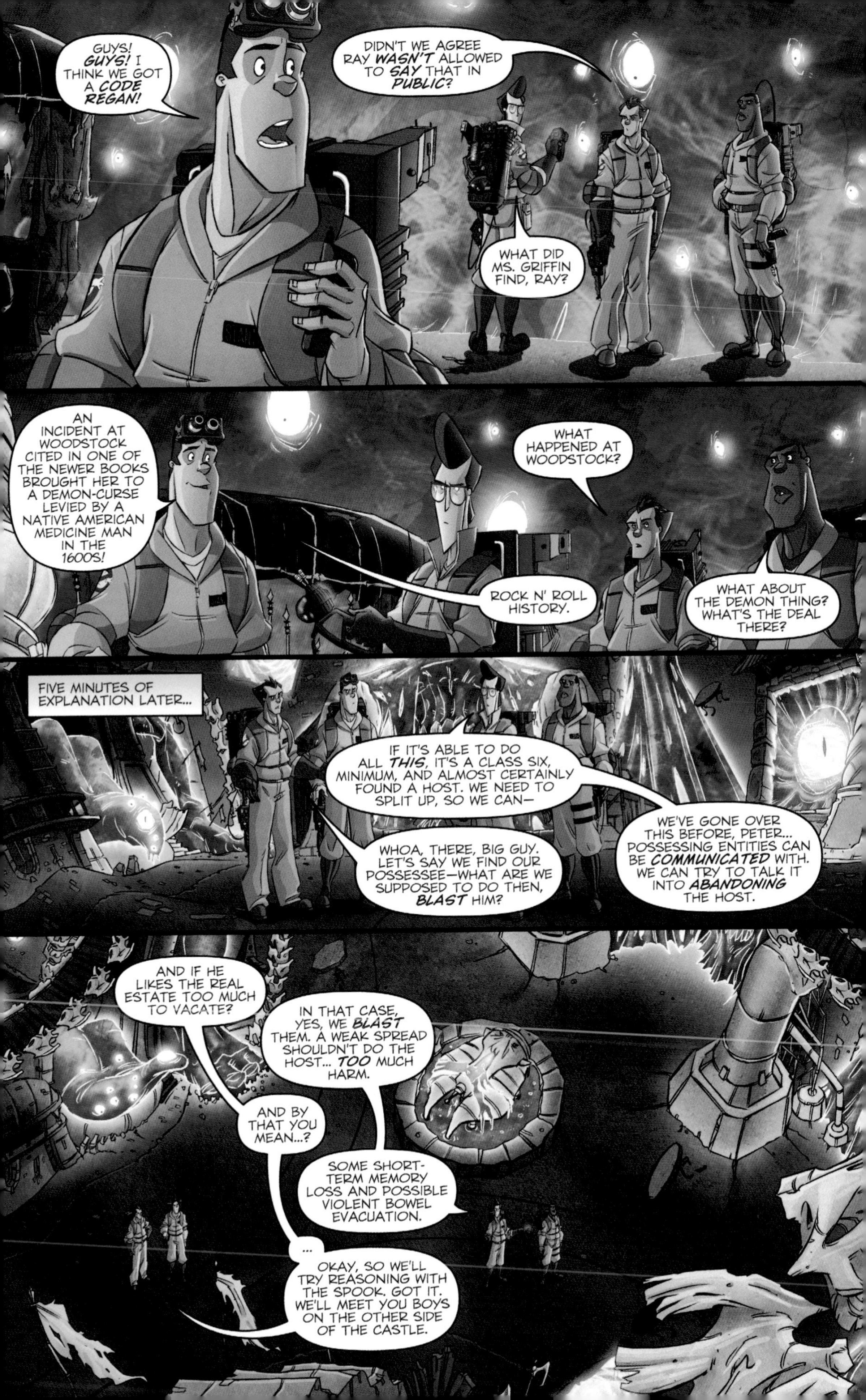
GUYS! GUYS! I THINK WE GOT A CODE REGAN!
DIDN'T WE AGREE RAY WASN'T ALLOWED TO SAY THAT IN PUBLIC?
WHAT DID MS. GRIFFIN FIND, RAY?
AN INCIDENT AT WOODSTOCK CITED IN ONE OF THE NEWER BOOKS BROUGHT HER TO A DEMON-CURSE LEVIED BY A NATIVE AMERICAN MEDICINE MAN IN THE 1600S!
WHAT HAPPENED AT WOODSTOCK?
ROCK N' ROLL HISTORY.
WHAT ABOUT THE DEMON THING? WHAT'S THE DEAL THERE?
FIVE MINUTES OF EXPLANATION LATER...
IF IT'S ABLE TO DO ALL THIS, IT'S A CLASS SIX, MINIMUM, AND ALMOST CERTAINLY FOUND A HOST. WE NEED TO SPLIT UP, SO WE CAN—
WHOA, THERE, BIG GUY. LET'S SAY WE FIND OUR POSSESSEE—WHAT ARE WE SUPPOSED TO DO THEN, BLAST HIM?
WE'VE GONE OVER THIS BEFORE, PETER... POSSESSING ENTITIES CAN BE COMMUNICATED WITH. WE CAN TRY TO TALK IT INTO ABANDONING THE HOST.
AND IF HE LIKES THE REAL ESTATE TOO MUCH TO VACATE?
IN THAT CASE, YES, WE BLAST THEM. A WEAK SPREAD SHOULDN'T DO THE HOST... TOO MUCH HARM.
AND BY THAT YOU MEAN...?
SOME SHORT-TERM MEMORY LOSS AND POSSIBLE VIOLENT BOWEL EVACUATION.
...
OKAY, SO WE'LL TRY REASONING WITH THE SPOOK. GOT IT. WE'LL MEET YOU BOYS ON THE OTHER SIDE OF THE CASTLE.

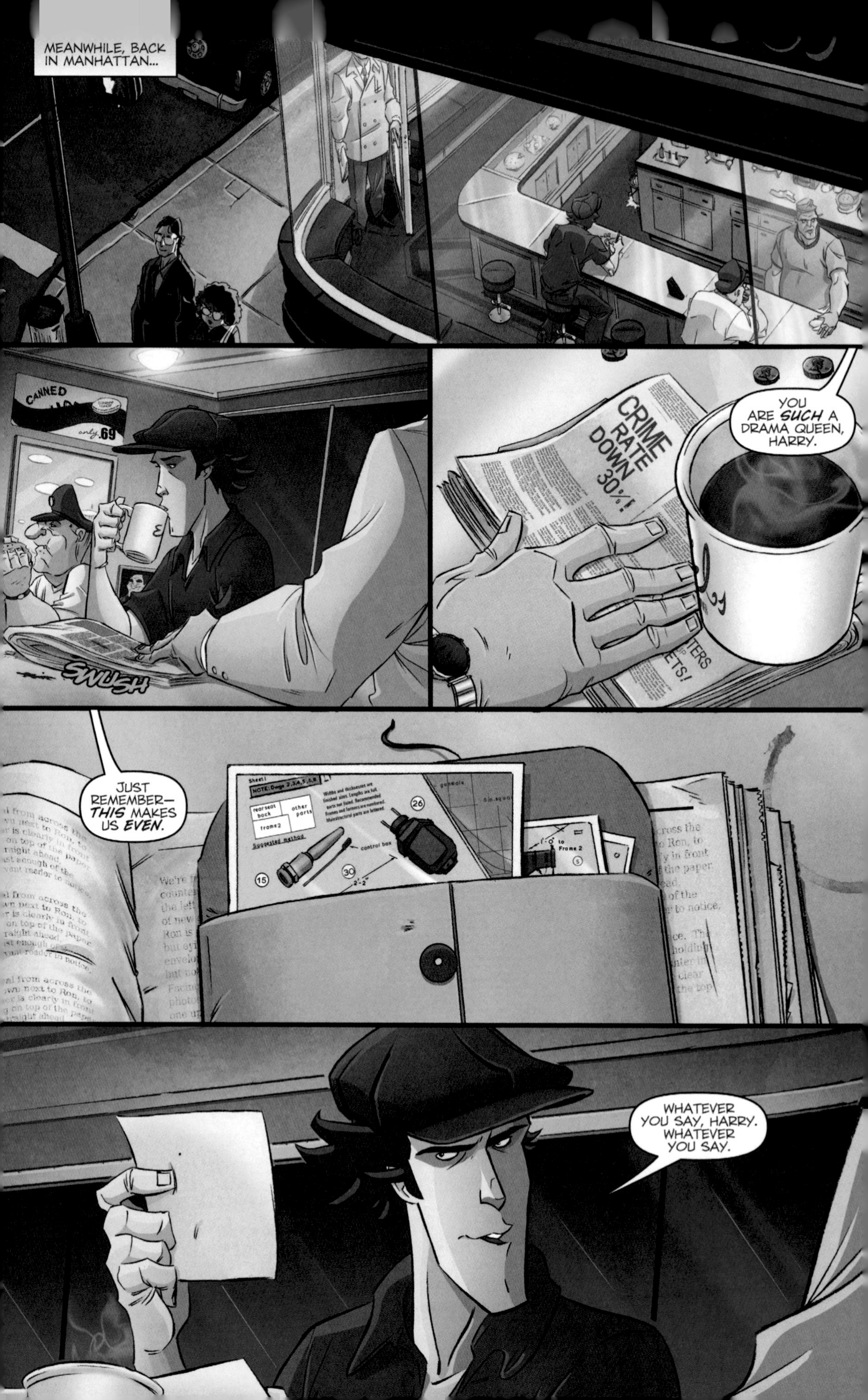
MEANWHILE, BACK IN MANHATTAN...
CANNED
only .69
SWUSH
CRIME RATE DOWN 30%!
YOU ARE SUCH A DRAMA QUEEN, HARRY.
JUST REMEMBER— THIS MAKES US EVEN.
WHATEVER YOU SAY, HARRY. WHATEVER YOU SAY.

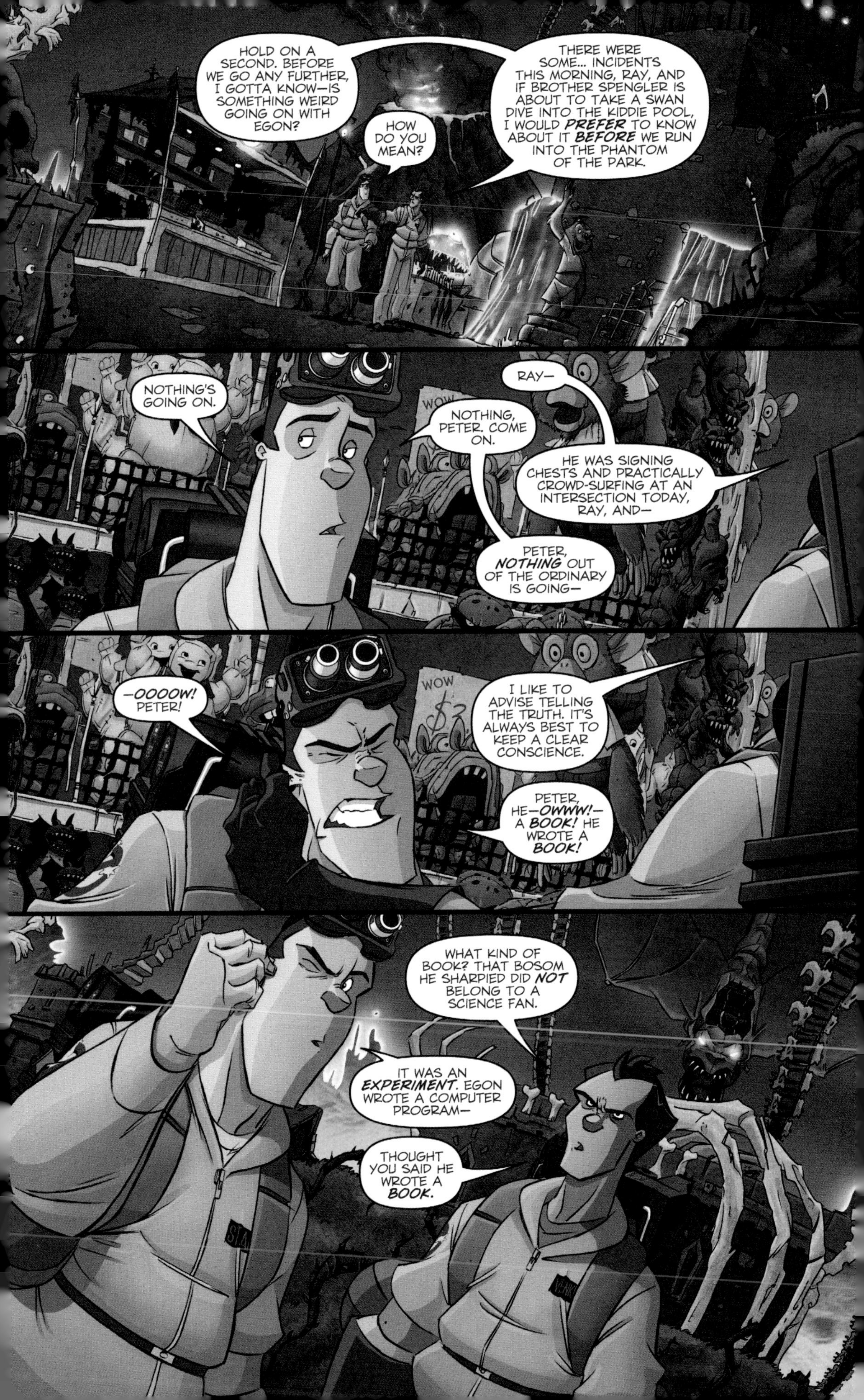
HOLD ON A SECOND. BEFORE WE GO ANY FURTHER, I GOTTA KNOW—IS SOMETHING WEIRD GOING ON WITH EGON?
HOW DO YOU MEAN?
THERE WERE SOME... INCIDENTS THIS MORNING, RAY, AND IF BROTHER SPENGLER IS ABOUT TO TAKE A SWAN DIVE INTO THE KIDDIE POOL, I WOULD **PREFER** TO KNOW ABOUT IT **BEFORE** WE RUN INTO THE PHANTOM OF THE PARK.
NOTHING'S GOING ON.
RAY—
NOTHING, PETER. COME ON.
HE WAS SIGNING CHESTS AND PRACTICALLY CROWD-SURFING AT AN INTERSECTION TODAY, RAY, AND—
PETER, **NOTHING** OUT OF THE ORDINARY IS GOING—
—OOOOW! PETER!
WOW
I LIKE TO ADVISE TELLING THE TRUTH. IT'S ALWAYS BEST TO KEEP A CLEAR CONSCIENCE.
PETER, HE—**OWWW!**— A **BOOK!** HE WROTE A **BOOK!**
WHAT KIND OF BOOK? THAT BOSOM HE SHARPIED DID **NOT** BELONG TO A SCIENCE FAN.
IT WAS AN **EXPERIMENT**. EGON WROTE A COMPUTER PROGRAM—
THOUGHT YOU SAID HE WROTE A **BOOK.**

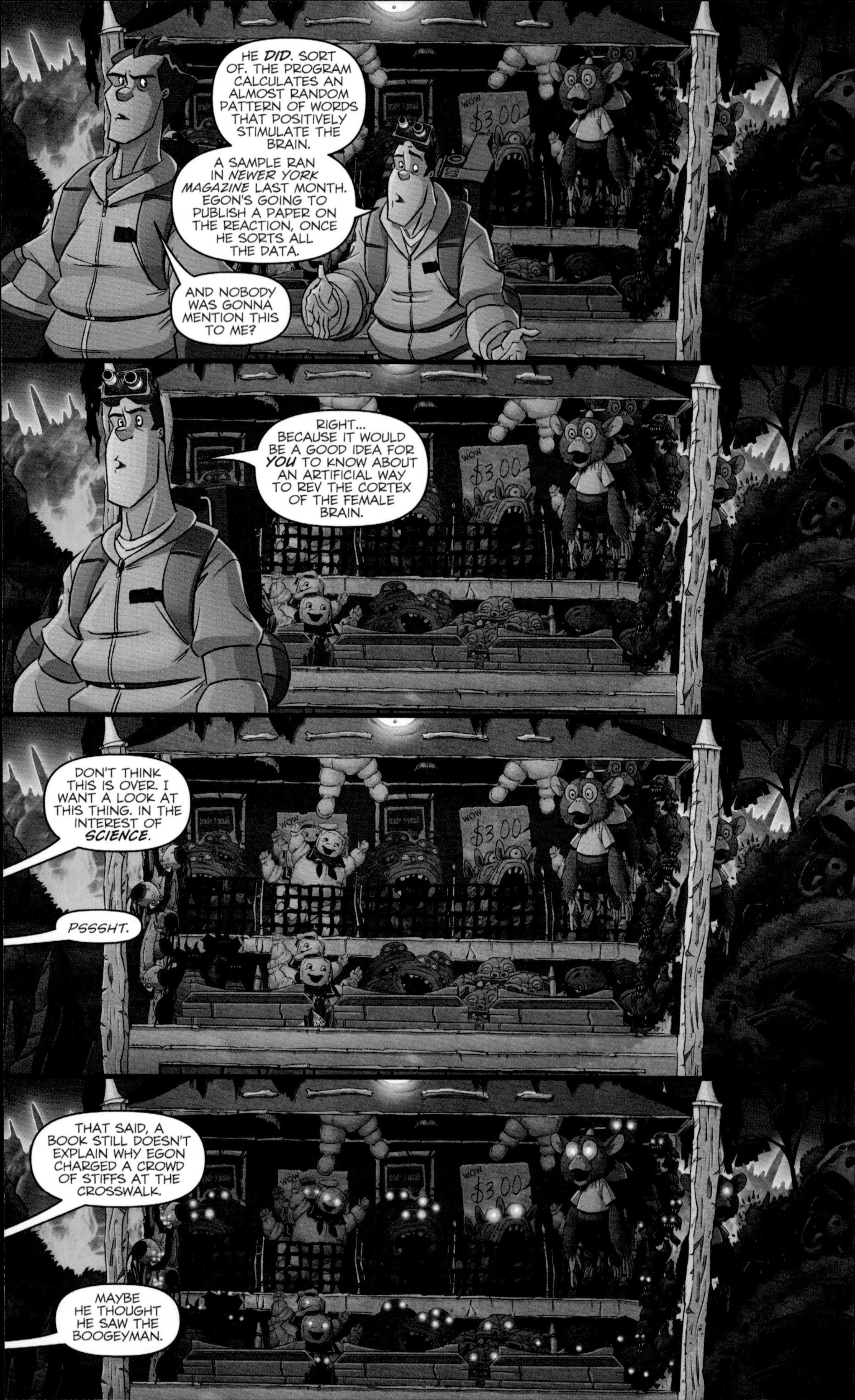
HE DID. SORT OF. THE PROGRAM CALCULATES AN ALMOST RANDOM PATTERN OF WORDS THAT POSITIVELY STIMULATE THE BRAIN.
A SAMPLE RAN IN NEWER YORK MAGAZINE LAST MONTH. EGON'S GOING TO PUBLISH A PAPER ON THE REACTION, ONCE HE SORTS ALL THE DATA.
AND NOBODY WAS GONNA MENTION THIS TO ME?
WOW
$3.00
RIGHT... BECAUSE IT WOULD BE A GOOD IDEA FOR YOU TO KNOW ABOUT AN ARTIFICIAL WAY TO REV THE CORTEX OF THE FEMALE BRAIN.
DON'T THINK THIS IS OVER. I WANT A LOOK AT THIS THING. IN THE INTEREST OF SCIENCE.
PSSSHT.
THAT SAID, A BOOK STILL DOESN'T EXPLAIN WHY EGON CHARGED A CROWD OF STIFFS AT THE CROSSWALK.
MAYBE HE THOUGHT HE SAW THE BOOGEYMAN.

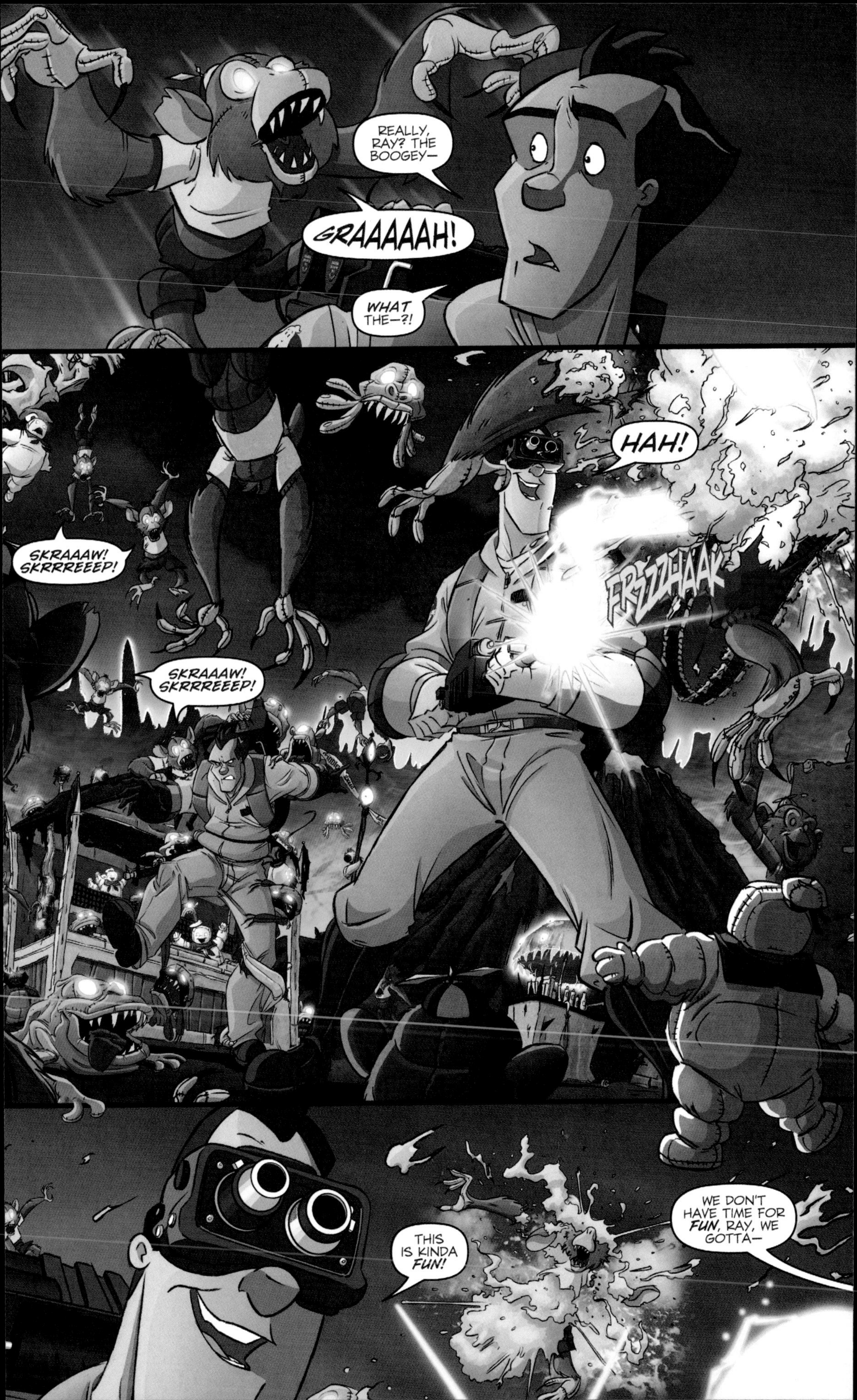
REALLY, RAY? THE BOOGEY—
GRAAAAAH!
WHAT THE—?!
HAH!
SKRAAAW! SKRRREEEP!
SKRAAAW! SKRRREEEP!
FRZZZHAAK
THIS IS KINDA FUN!
WE DON'T HAVE TIME FOR FUN, RAY, WE GOTTA—

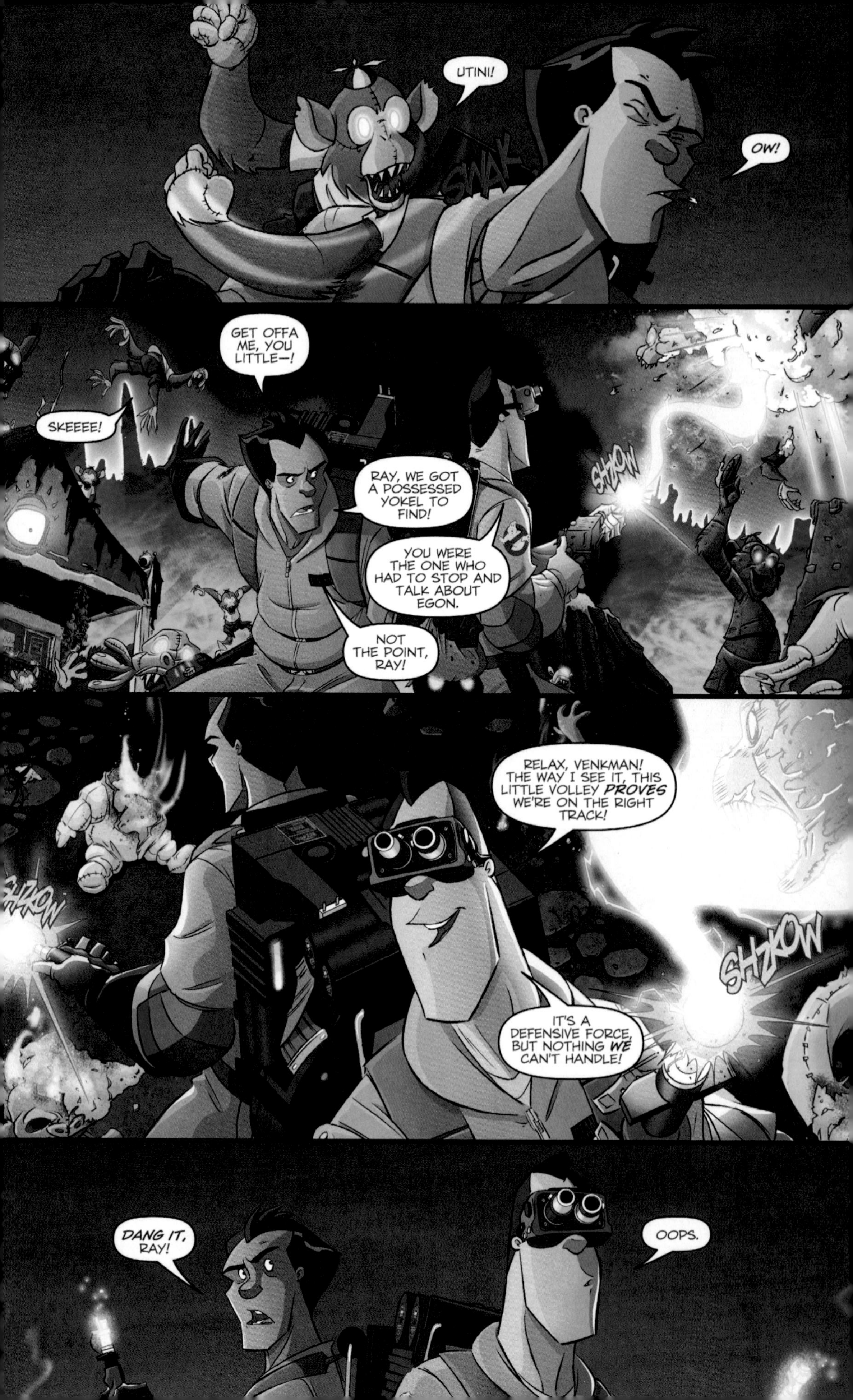
UTINI!
SWAK
OW!
GET OFFA ME, YOU LITTLE—!
SKEEEE!
RAY, WE GOT A POSSESSED YOKEL TO FIND!
SHZKOW
YOU WERE THE ONE WHO HAD TO STOP AND TALK ABOUT EGON.
NOT THE POINT, RAY!
RELAX, VENKMAN! THE WAY I SEE IT, THIS LITTLE VOLLEY PROVES WE'RE ON THE RIGHT TRACK!
SHZKOW
SHZKOW
IT'S A DEFENSIVE FORCE, BUT NOTHING WE CAN'T HANDLE!
DANG IT, RAY!
OOPS.

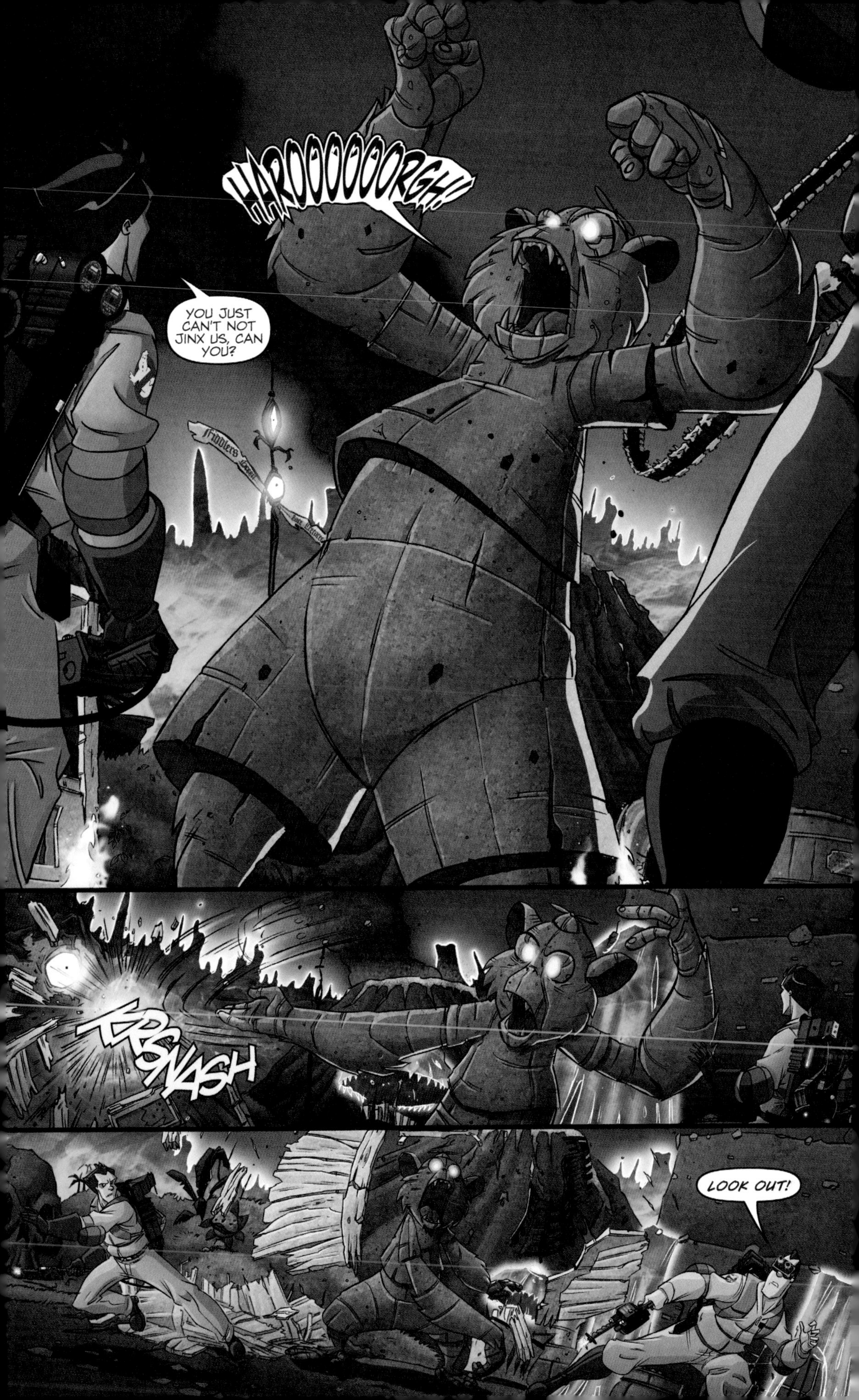
HAROOOOOORGH!!
YOU JUST CAN'T NOT JINX US, CAN YOU?
KRSNASH
LOOK OUT!

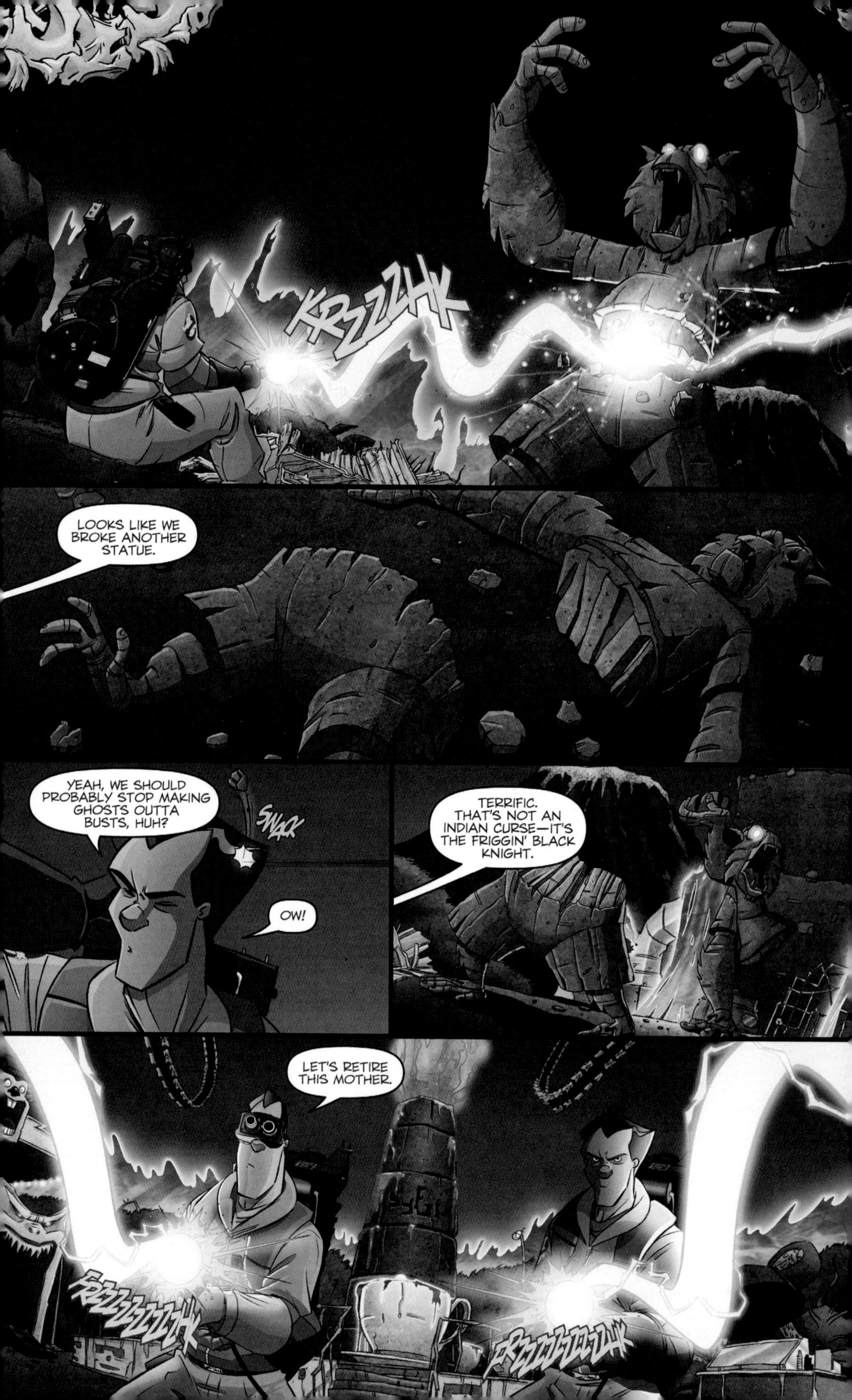
KRZZZZHK
LOOKS LIKE WE BROKE ANOTHER STATUE.
YEAH, WE SHOULD PROBABLY STOP MAKING GHOSTS OUTTA BUSTS, HUH?
SWACK
OW!
TERRIFIC. THAT'S NOT AN INDIAN CURSE—IT'S THE FRIGGIN' BLACK KNIGHT.
LET'S RETIRE THIS MOTHER.

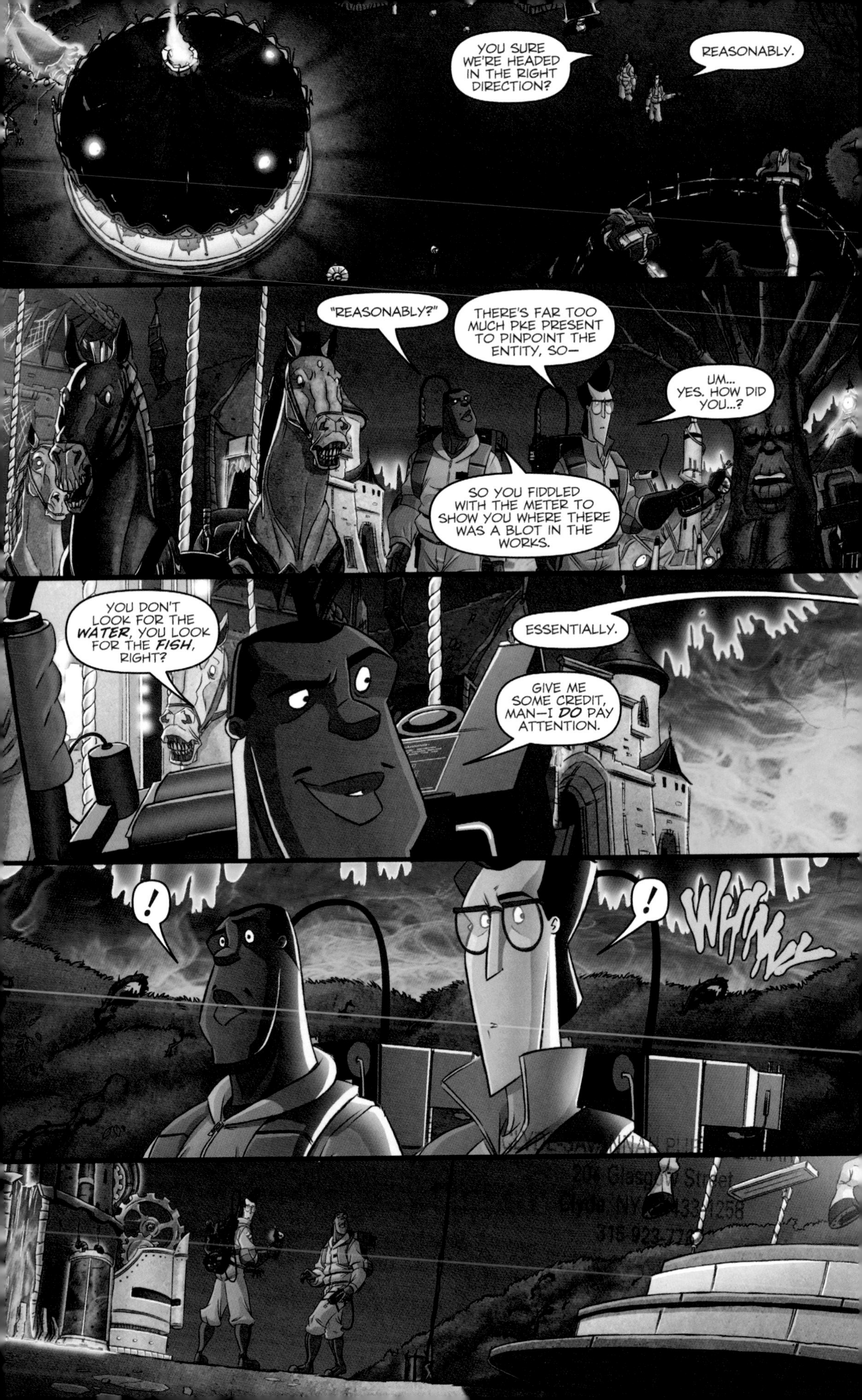
YOU SURE WE'RE HEADED IN THE RIGHT DIRECTION?
REASONABLY.
"REASONABLY?"
THERE'S FAR TOO MUCH PKE PRESENT TO PINPOINT THE ENTITY, SO—
SO YOU FIDDLED WITH THE METER TO SHOW YOU WHERE THERE WAS A BLOT IN THE WORKS.
UM... YES. HOW DID YOU...?
YOU DON'T LOOK FOR THE ***WATER***, YOU LOOK FOR THE ***FISH***, RIGHT?
ESSENTIALLY.
GIVE ME SOME CREDIT, MAN—I ***DO*** PAY ATTENTION.
!
!
WHINNY

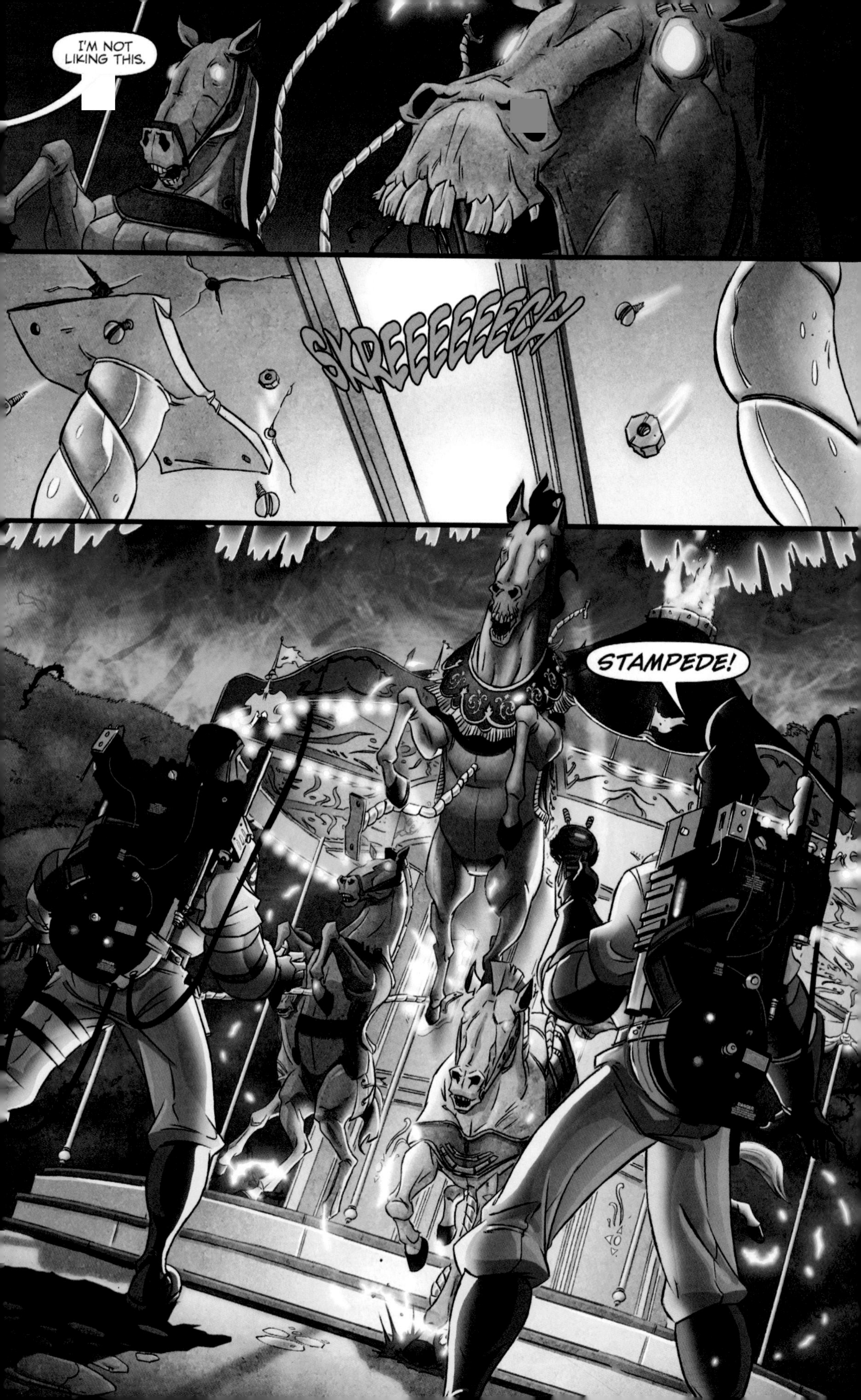
I'M NOT LIKING THIS.
SKREEEEEECH
STAMPEDE!

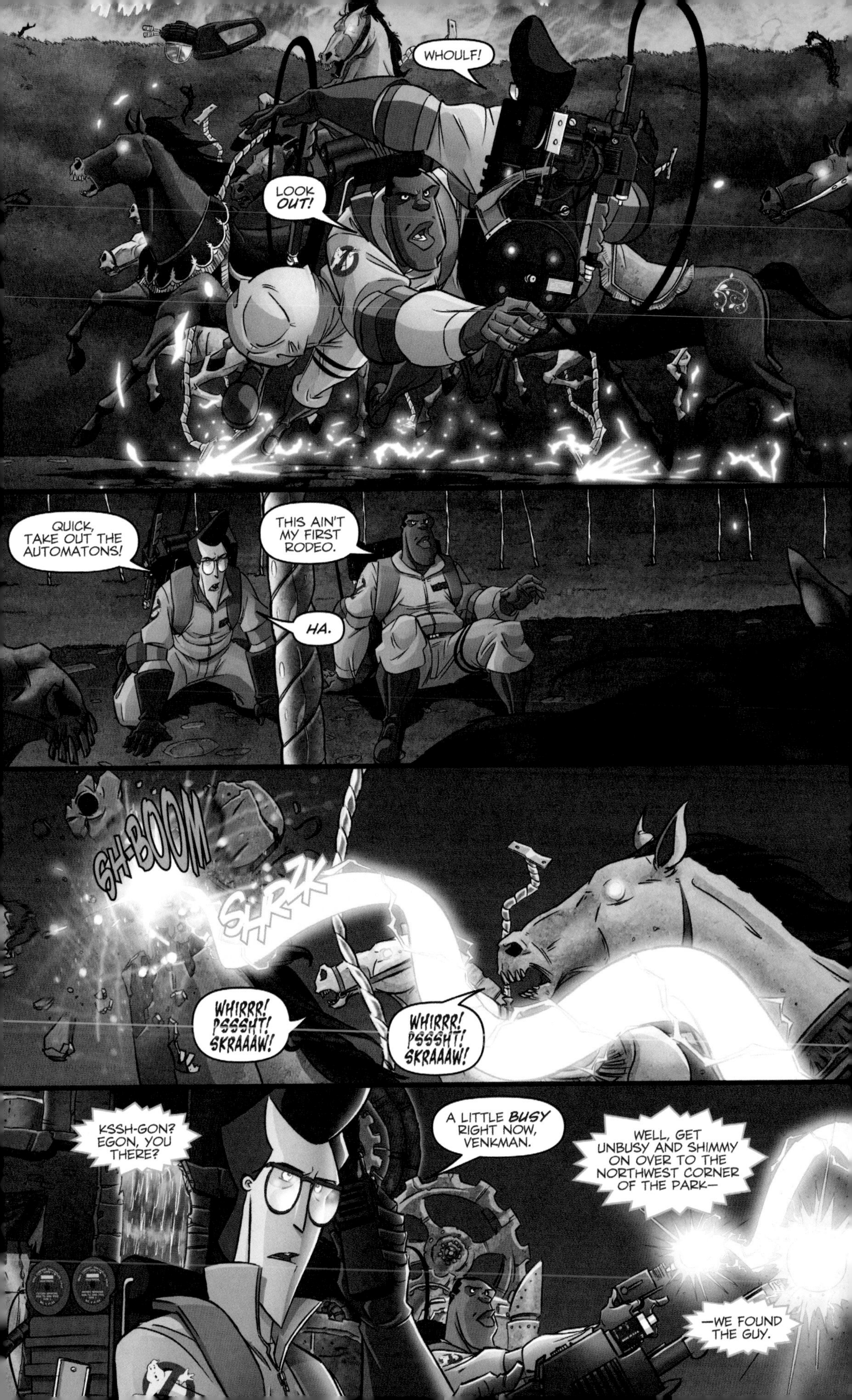
WHOULF!
LOOK OUT!
QUICK, TAKE OUT THE AUTOMATONS!
THIS AIN'T MY FIRST RODEO.
HA.
SH-BOOM
SHRZK
WHIRRR! PSSSHT! SKRAAAW!
WHIRRR! PSSSHT! SKRAAAW!
KSSH-GON? EGON, YOU THERE?
A LITTLE BUSY RIGHT NOW, VENKMAN.
WELL, GET UNBUSY AND SHIMMY ON OVER TO THE NORTHWEST CORNER OF THE PARK—
—WE FOUND THE GUY.

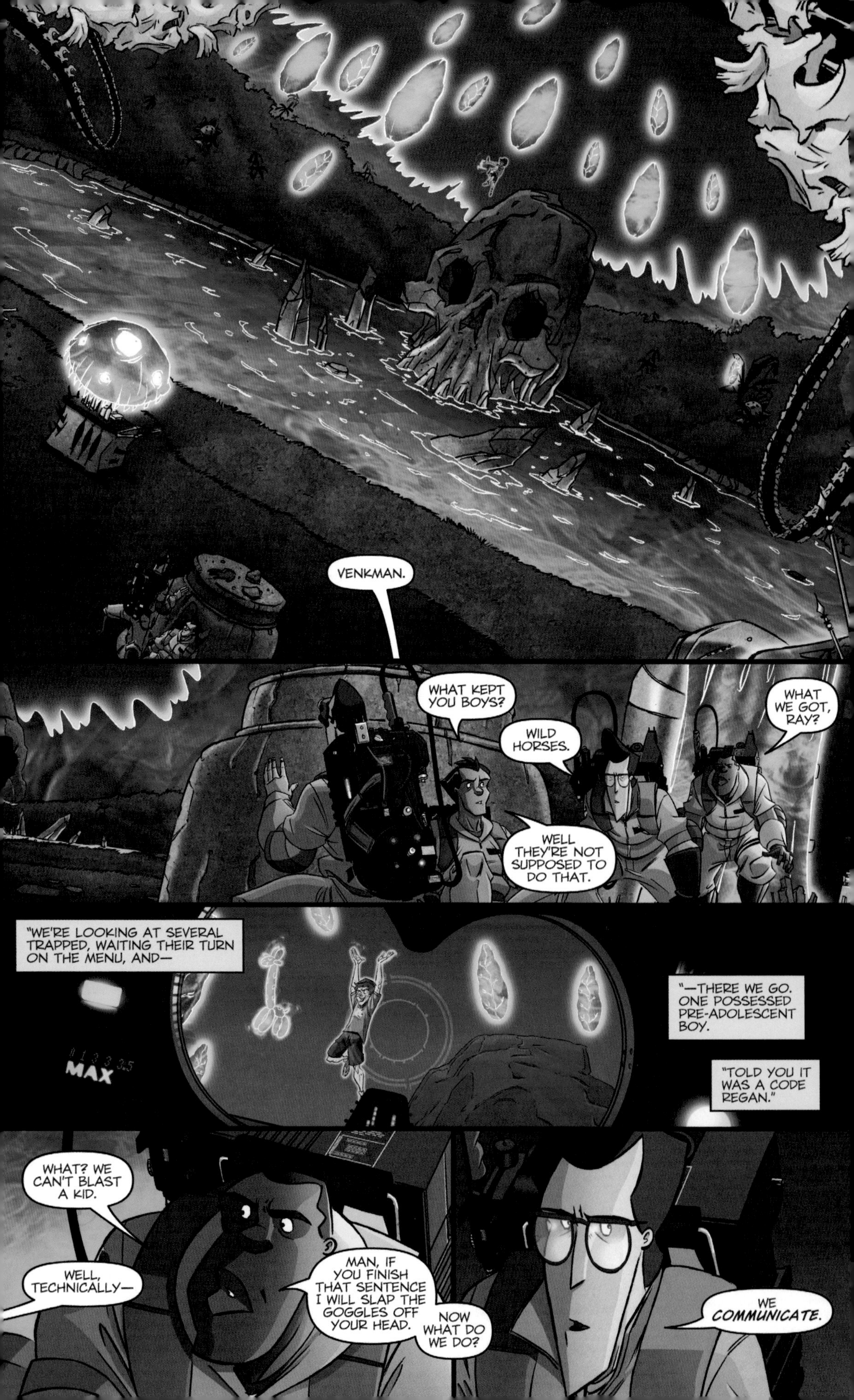
VENKMAN.
WHAT KEPT YOU BOYS?
WILD HORSES.
WELL THEY'RE NOT SUPPOSED TO DO THAT.
WHAT WE GOT, RAY?
"WE'RE LOOKING AT SEVERAL TRAPPED, WAITING THEIR TURN ON THE MENU, AND—
"—THERE WE GO. ONE POSSESSED PRE-ADOLESCENT BOY.
"TOLD YOU IT WAS A CODE REGAN."
MAX
WHAT? WE CAN'T BLAST A KID.
WELL, TECHNICALLY—
MAN, IF YOU FINISH THAT SENTENCE I WILL SLAP THE GOGGLES OFF YOUR HEAD.
NOW WHAT DO WE DO?
WE *COMMUNICATE*.

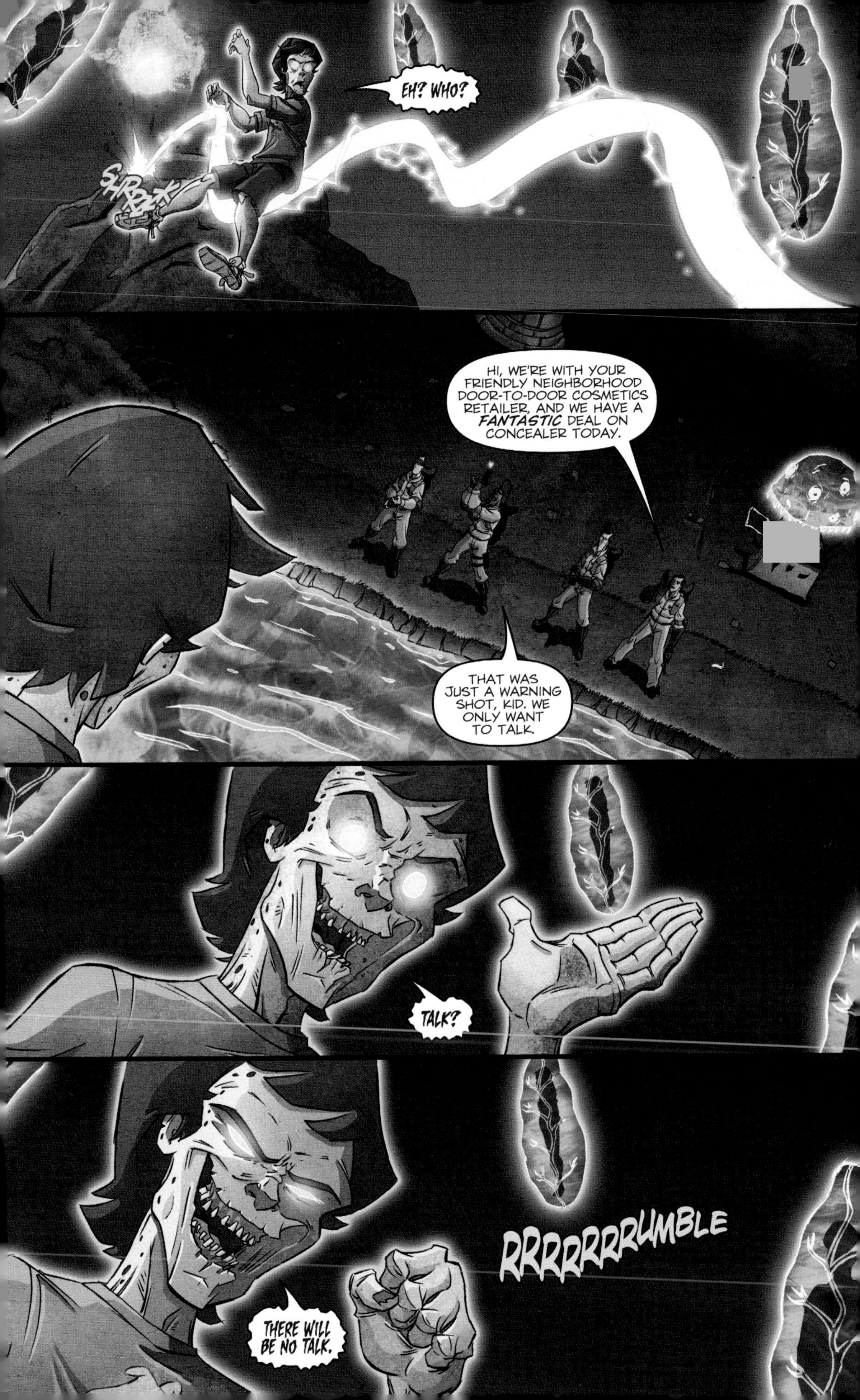
EH? WHO?
SHRZZK
HI, WE'RE WITH YOUR FRIENDLY NEIGHBORHOOD DOOR-TO-DOOR COSMETICS RETAILER, AND WE HAVE A *FANTASTIC* DEAL ON CONCEALER TODAY.
THAT WAS JUST A WARNING SHOT, KID. WE ONLY WANT TO TALK.
TALK?
RRRRRRRUMBLE
THERE WILL BE NO TALK.

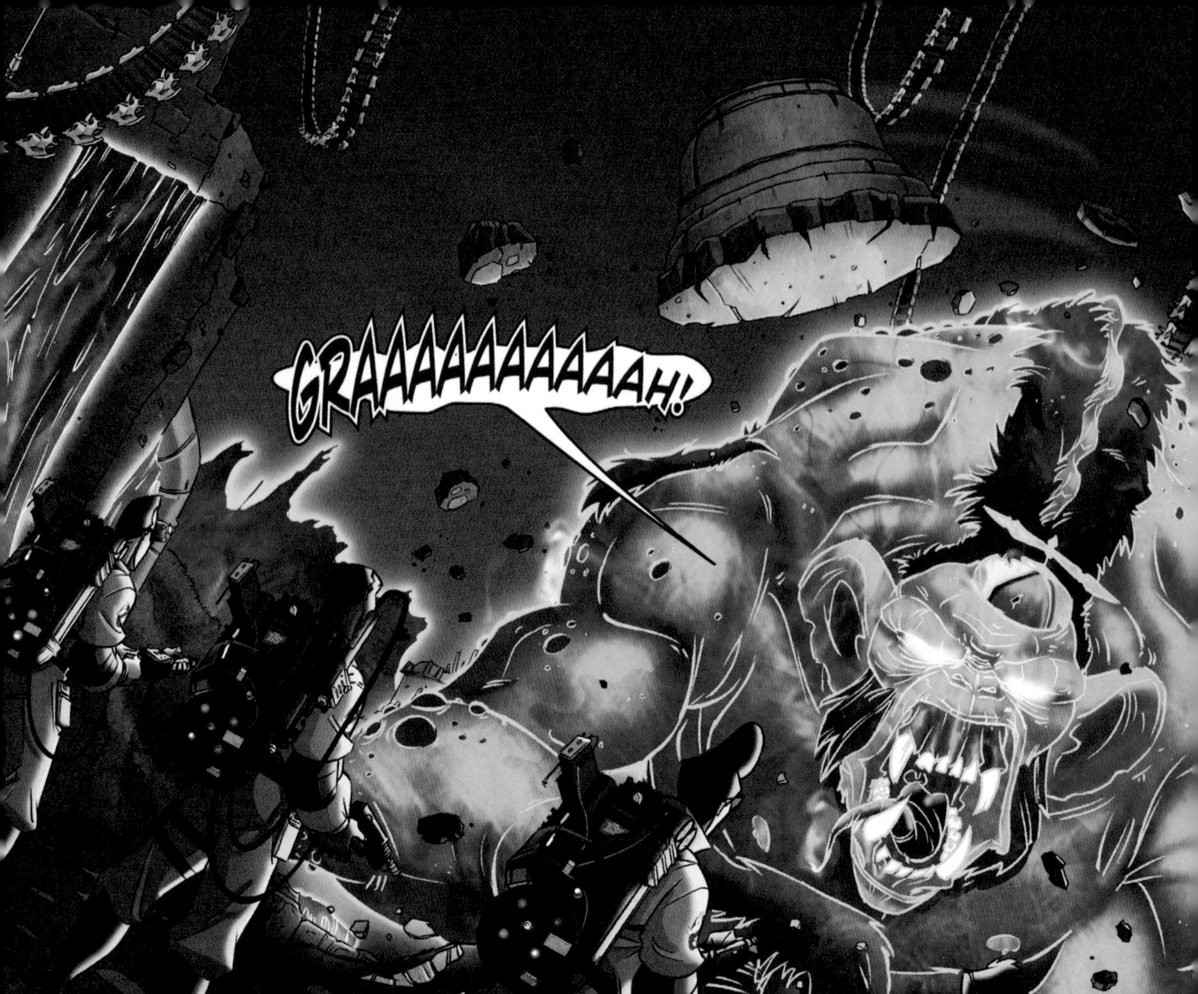
GRAAAAAAAAAAH!

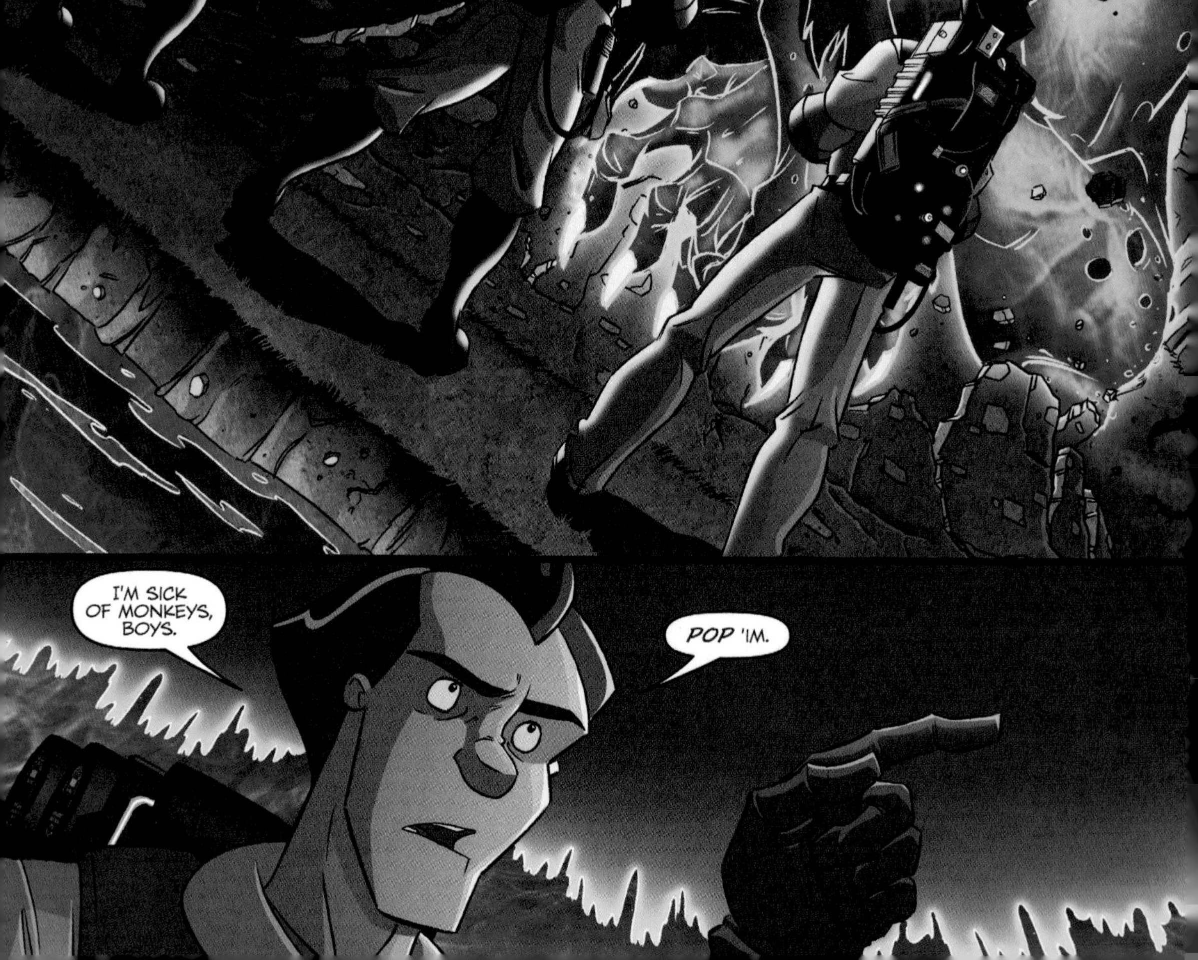
I'M SICK OF MONKEYS, BOYS.
POP 'IM.

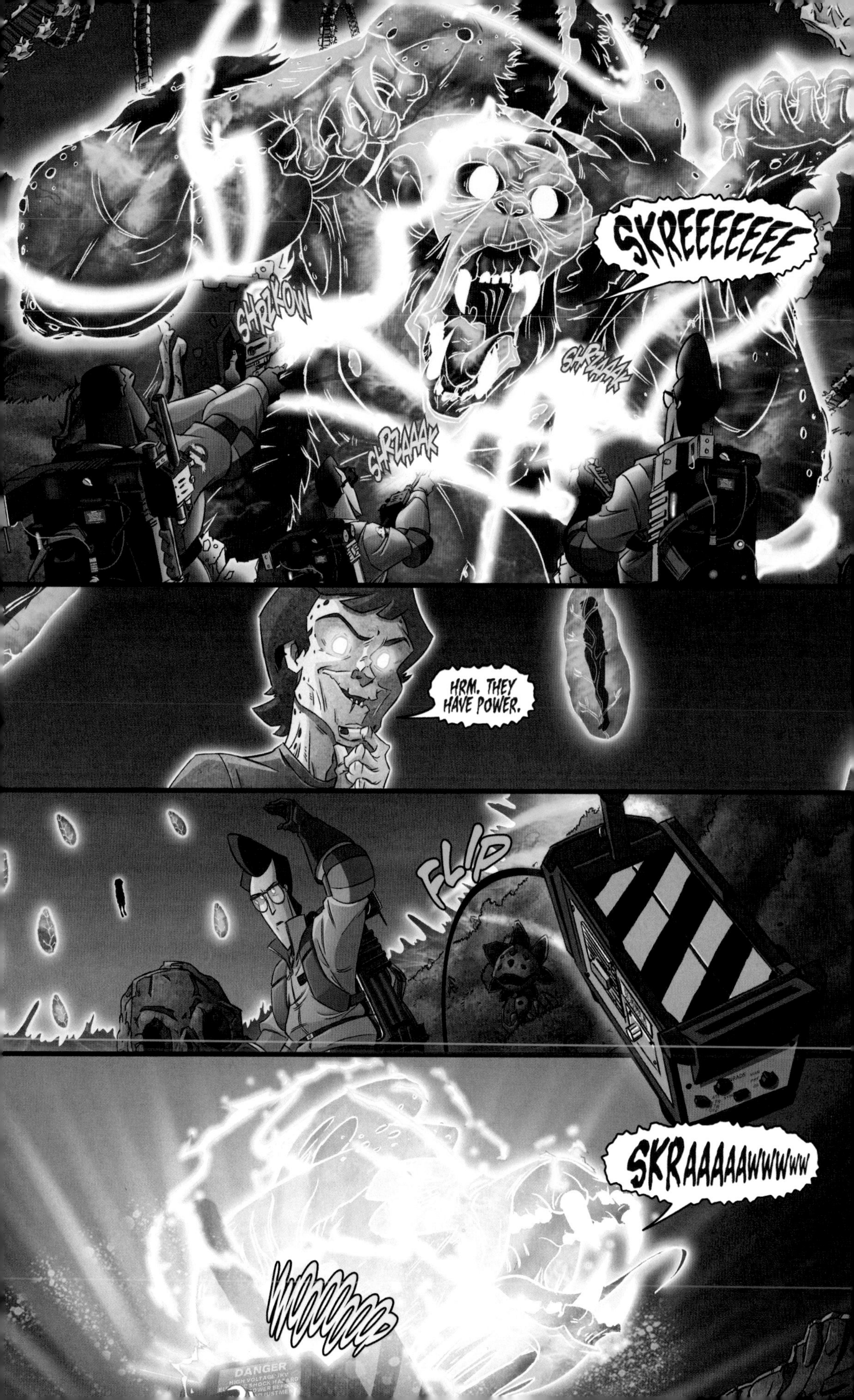
SKREEEEEEEE
SHZKOW
SHZAAAK
SHZAAAK
HRM. THEY HAVE POWER.
FLIP
SKRAAAAWWWWW
DANGER

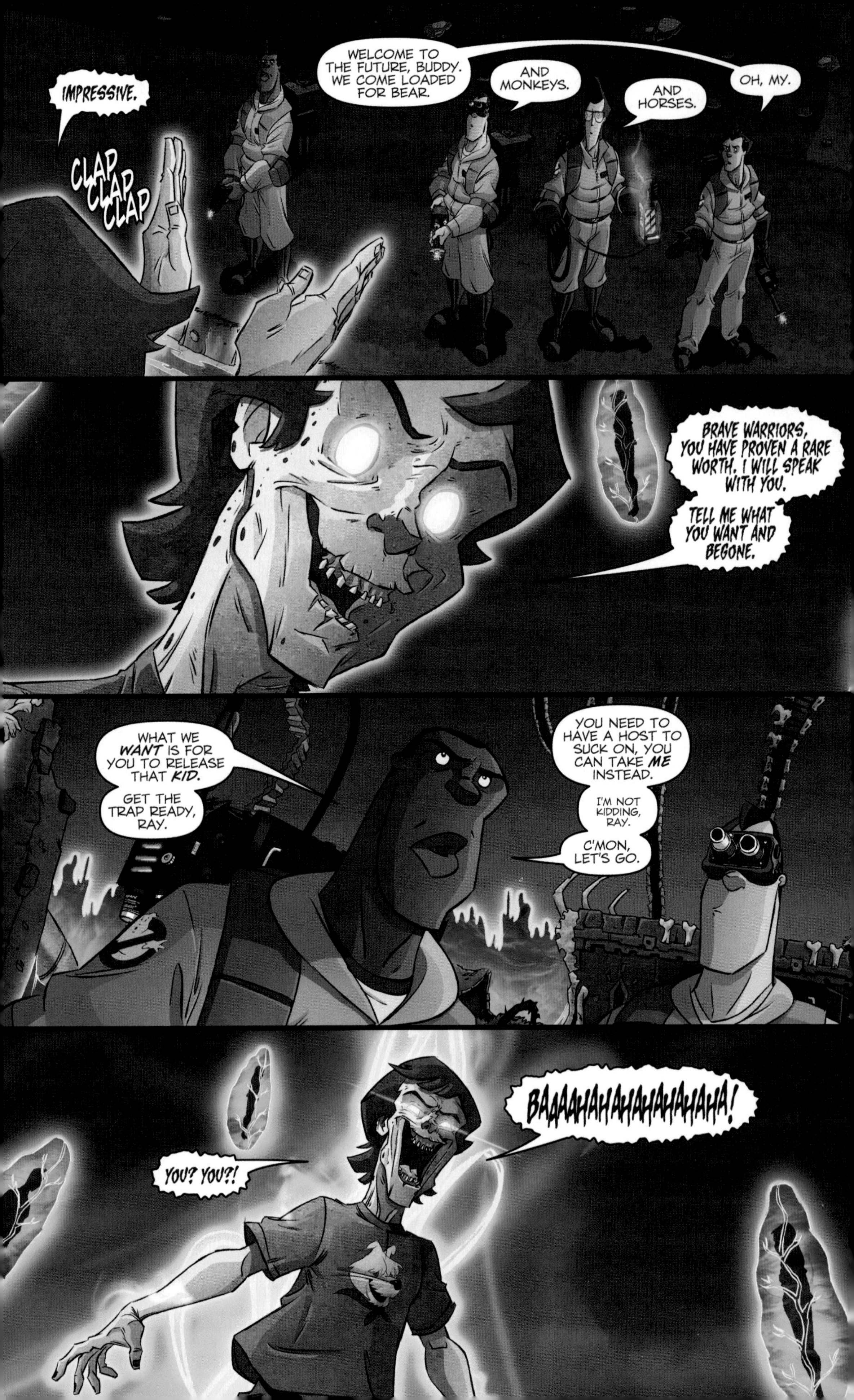

IMPRESSIVE.
CLAP CLAP CLAP
WELCOME TO THE FUTURE, BUDDY. WE COME LOADED FOR BEAR.
AND MONKEYS.
AND HORSES.
OH, MY.
BRAVE WARRIORS, YOU HAVE PROVEN A RARE WORTH. I WILL SPEAK WITH YOU.
TELL ME WHAT YOU WANT AND BEGONE.
WHAT WE WANT IS FOR YOU TO RELEASE THAT KID.
GET THE TRAP READY, RAY.
YOU NEED TO HAVE A HOST TO SUCK ON, YOU CAN TAKE ME INSTEAD.
I'M NOT KIDDING, RAY.
C'MON, LET'S GO.
YOU? YOU?!
BAAAAHAHAHAHAHAHAHA!

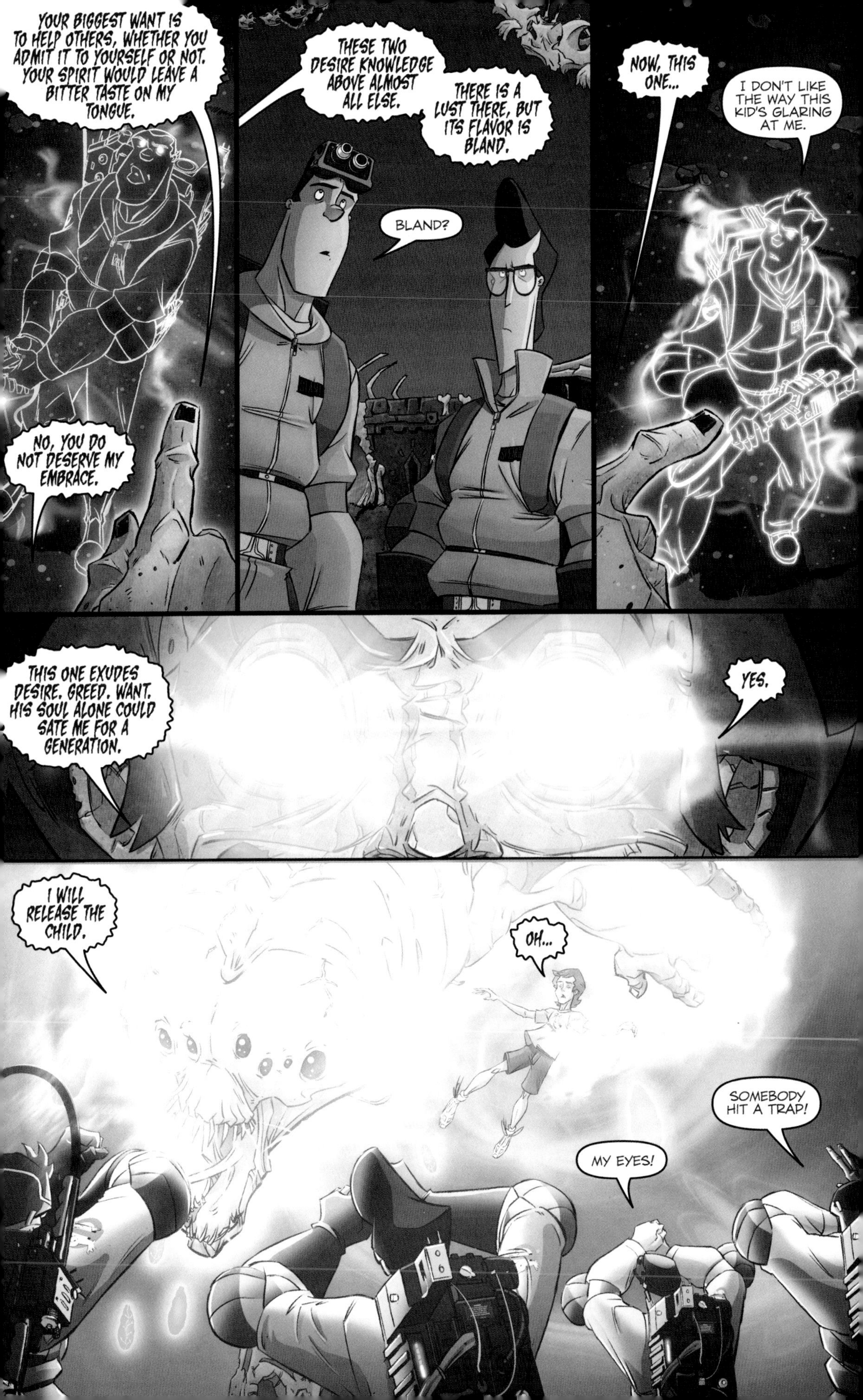
YOUR BIGGEST WANT IS TO HELP OTHERS, WHETHER YOU ADMIT IT TO YOURSELF OR NOT. YOUR SPIRIT WOULD LEAVE A BITTER TASTE ON MY TONGUE.
NO, YOU DO NOT DESERVE MY EMBRACE.
THESE TWO DESIRE KNOWLEDGE ABOVE ALMOST ALL ELSE.
THERE IS A LUST THERE, BUT ITS FLAVOR IS BLAND.
BLAND?
NOW, THIS ONE...
I DON'T LIKE THE WAY THIS KID'S GLARING AT ME.
THIS ONE EXUDES DESIRE. GREED. WANT. HIS SOUL ALONE COULD SATE ME FOR A GENERATION.
YES.
I WILL RELEASE THE CHILD.
OH...
MY EYES!
SOMEBODY HIT A TRAP!

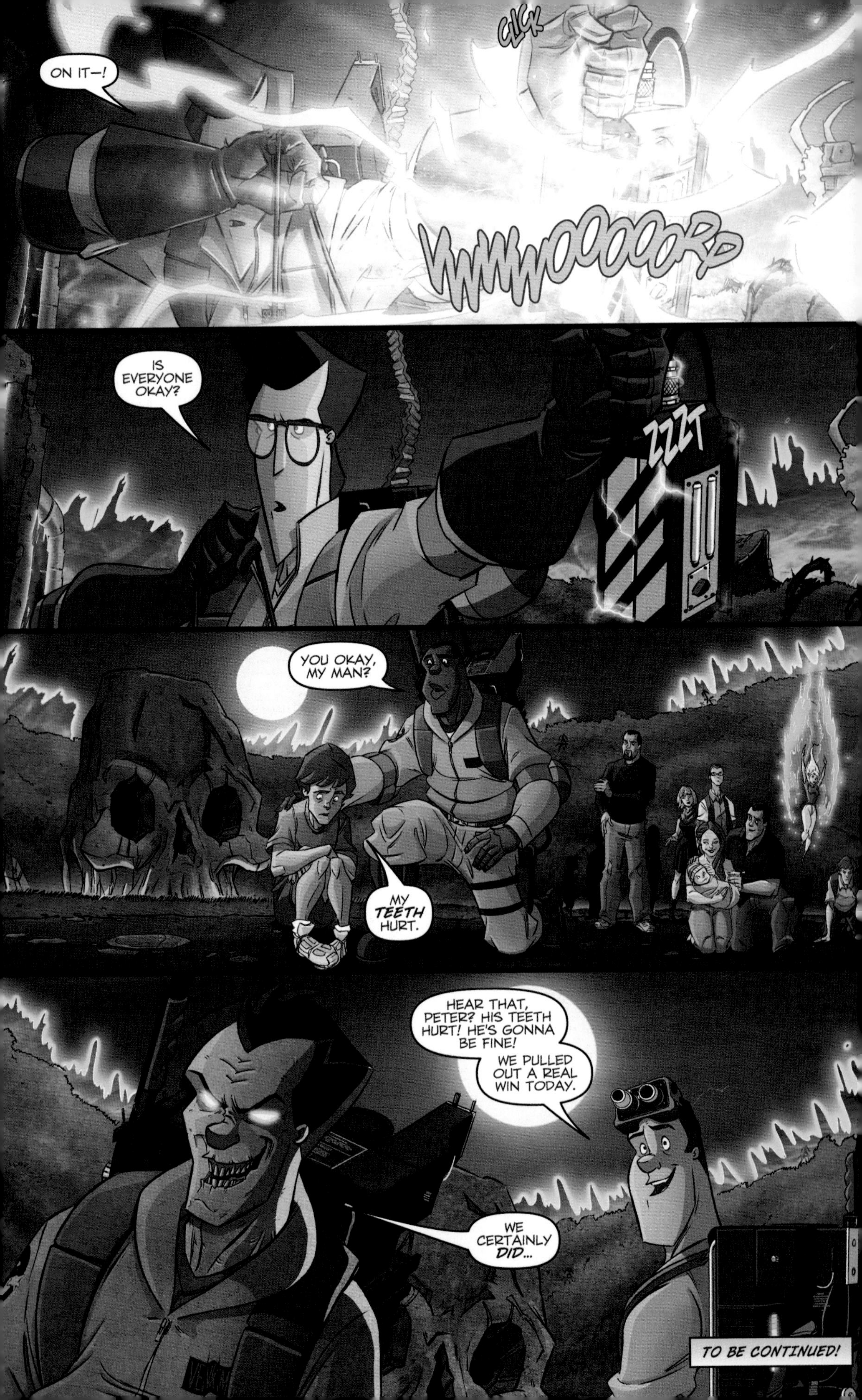

ON IT—!
CLICK
VWWWOOOOORP
IS EVERYONE OKAY?
ZZZT
YOU OKAY, MY MAN?
MY *TEETH* HURT.
HEAR THAT, PETER? HIS TEETH HURT! HE'S GONNA BE FINE!
WE PULLED OUT A REAL WIN TODAY.
WE CERTAINLY *DID*...
TO BE CONTINUED!

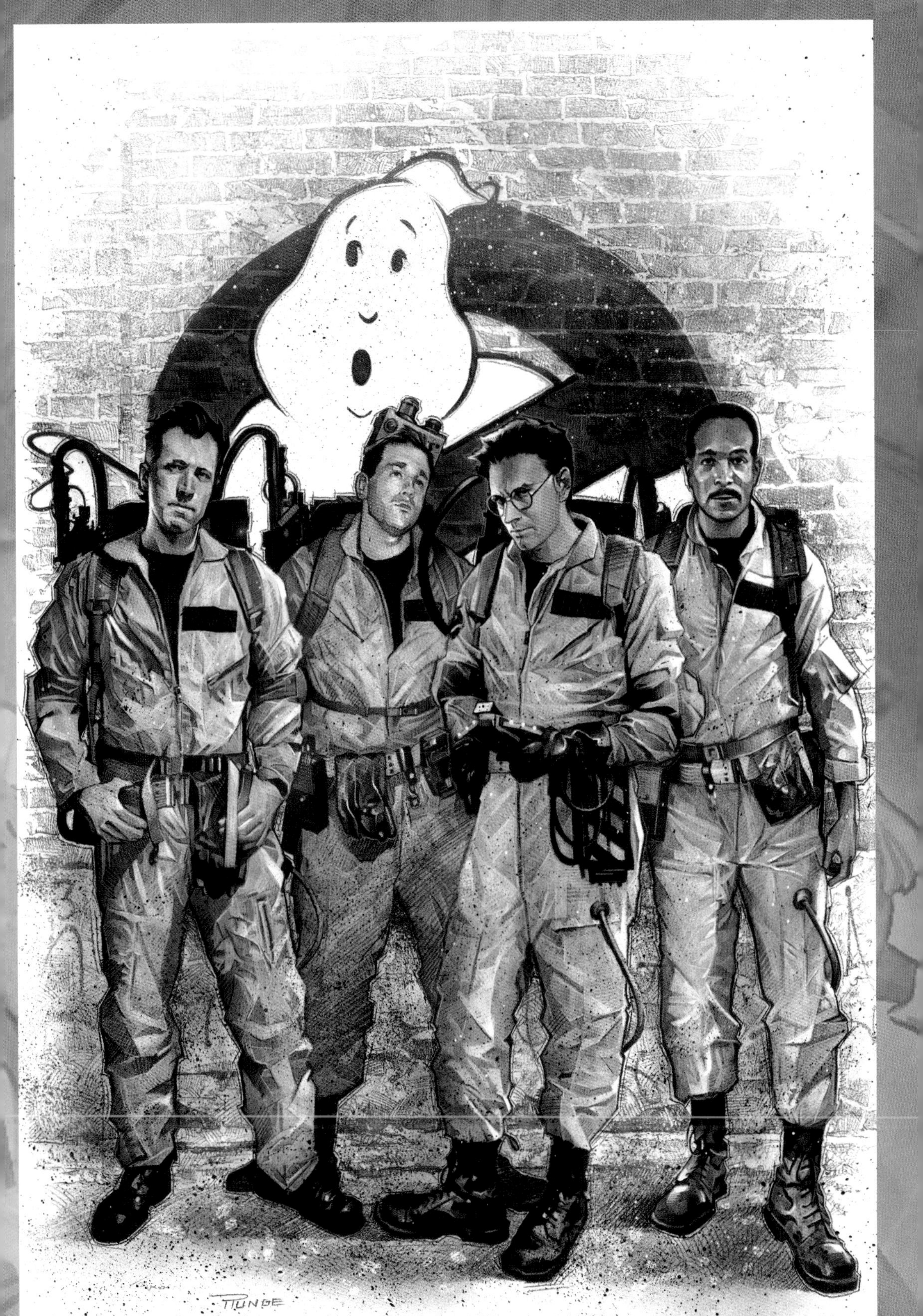
RUNGE

GHOSTBUSTERS ISSUE #6, COVER B
ART BY **NICK RUNGE**

GHOSTBUSTERS™

COLLECT THEM ALL!

Set of 12 Hardcover Books ISBN: 978-1-61479-484-4

Volume One: The Man from the Mirror, Parts 1–4

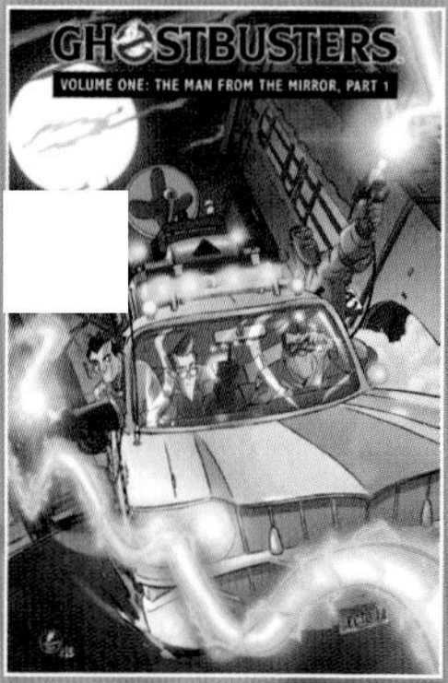
GHOSTBUSTERS
VOLUME ONE: THE MAN FROM THE MIRROR, PART 1

Hardcover Book ISBN
978-1-61479-485-1

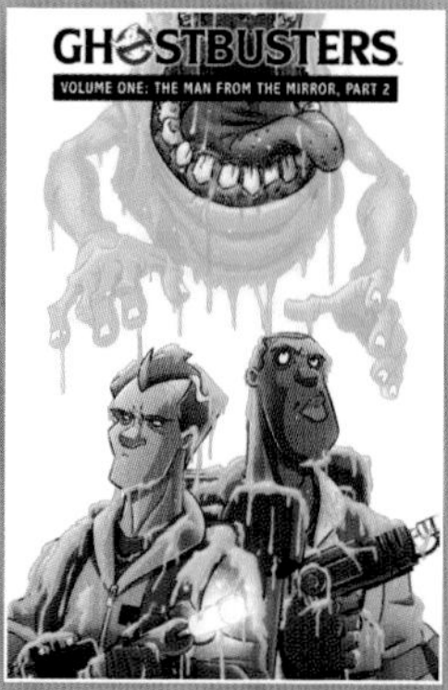
GHOSTBUSTERS
VOLUME ONE: THE MAN FROM THE MIRROR, PART 2

Hardcover Book ISBN
978-1-61479-486-8

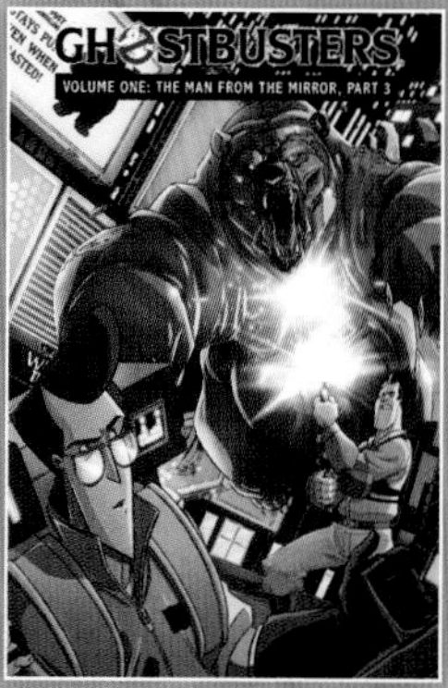
GHOSTBUSTERS
VOLUME ONE: THE MAN FROM THE MIRROR, PART 3

Hardcover Book ISBN
978-1-61479-487-5

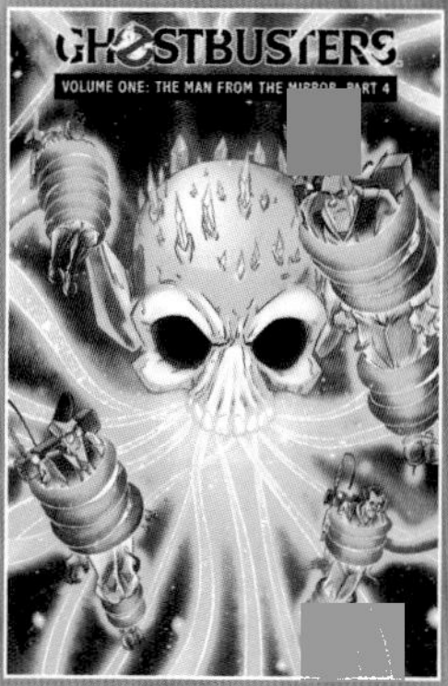
GHOSTBUSTERS

Hardcover Book ISBN
978-1-61479-488-2

Volume Two: The Most Magical Place on Earth, Parts 1–4

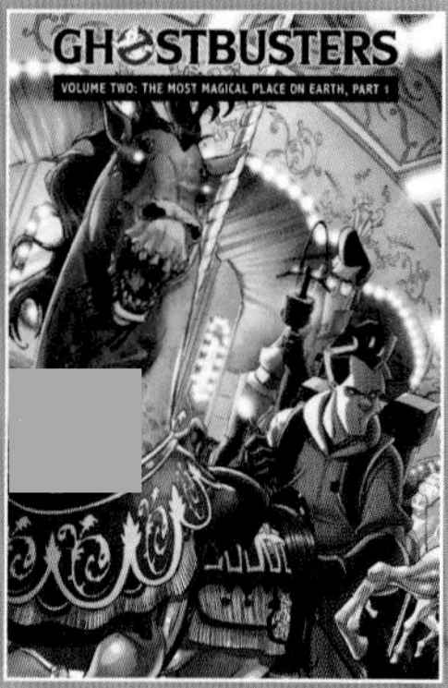
GHOSTBUSTERS
VOLUME TWO: THE MOST MAGICAL PLACE ON EARTH, PART 1

Hardcover Book ISBN
978-1-61479-489-9

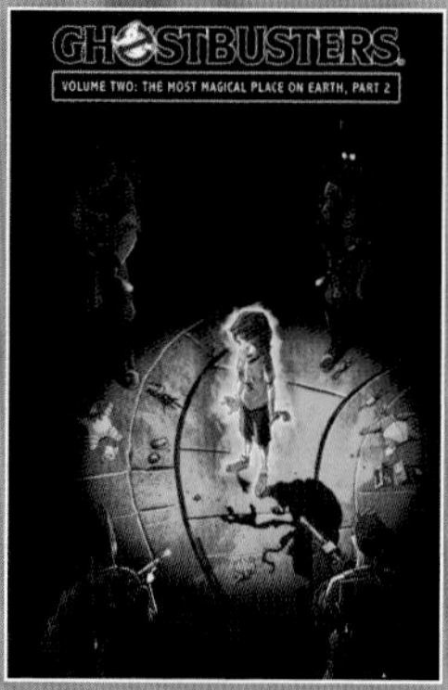
GHOSTBUSTERS
VOLUME TWO: THE MOST MAGICAL PLACE ON EARTH, PART 2

Hardcover Book ISBN
978-1-61479-490-5

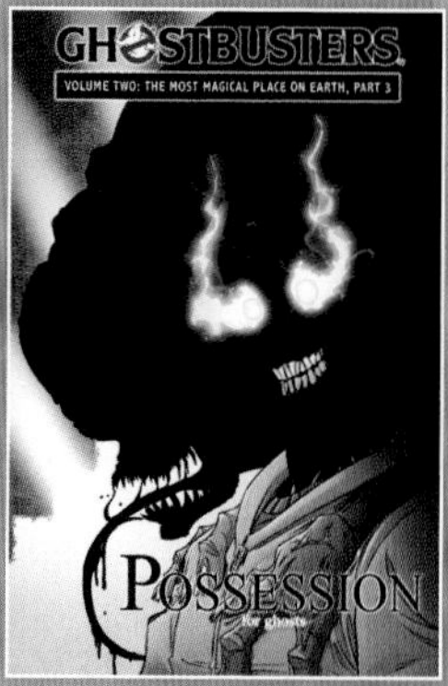
GHOSTBUSTERS
VOLUME TWO: THE MOST MAGICAL PLACE ON EARTH, PART 3
POSSESSION

Hardcover Book ISBN
978-1-61479-491-2

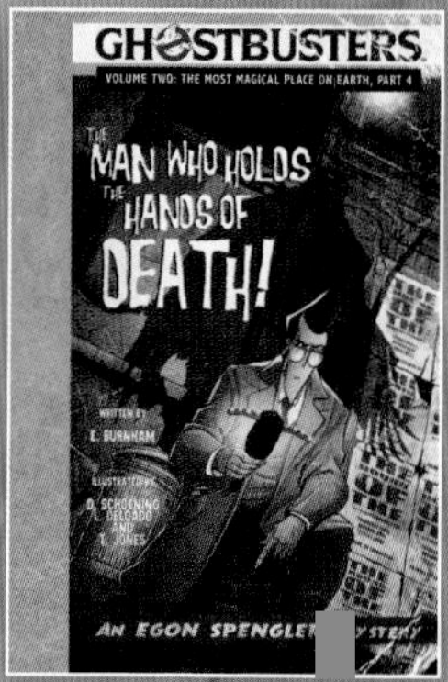
GHOSTBUSTERS
VOLUME TWO: THE MOST MAGICAL PLACE ON EARTH, PART 4
THE MAN WHO HOLDS THE HANDS OF DEATH!

Hardcover Book ISBN
978-1-61479-492-9

Volume Three: Haunted America, Parts 1–4

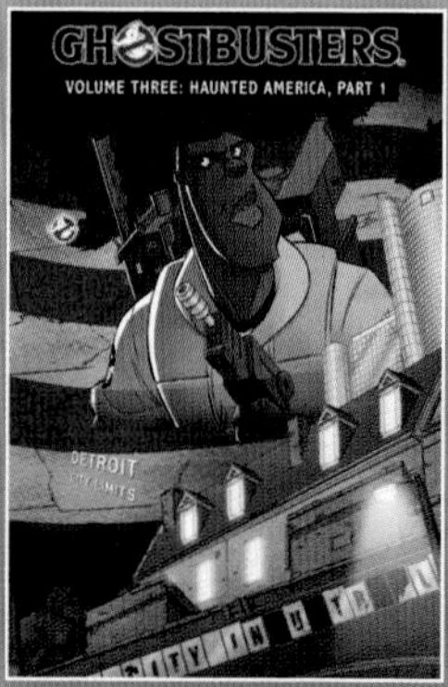
GHOSTBUSTERS
VOLUME THREE: HAUNTED AMERICA, PART 1
DETROIT

Hardcover Book ISBN
978-1-61479-493-6

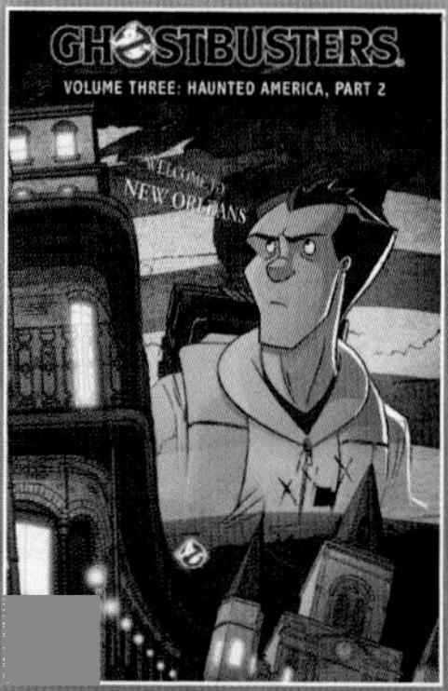
GHOSTBUSTERS
VOLUME THREE: HAUNTED AMERICA, PART 2

Hardcover Book ISBN
978-1-61479-494-3

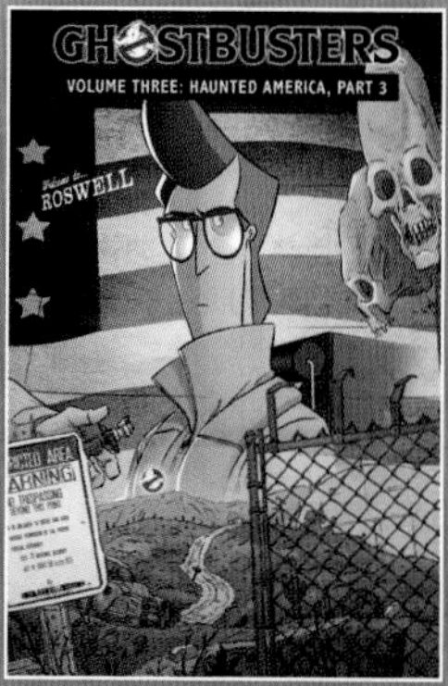
GHOSTBUSTERS
VOLUME THREE: HAUNTED AMERICA, PART 3
ROSWELL

Hardcover Book ISBN
978-1-61479-495-0

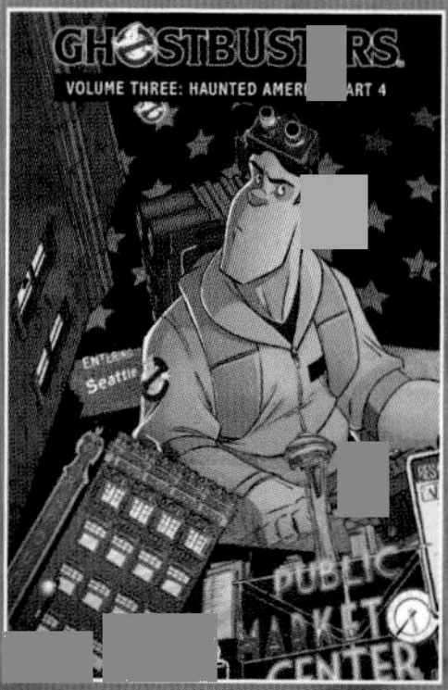
Seattle
PUBLIC MARKET CENTER

Hardcover Book ISBN
978-1-61479-496-7